THE NEW SINGLE DAD BILLIONAIRE

TINA GABOR

Copyright © 2022 by Tina Gabor

All rights reserved.

No part of this book may be reproduced in any form or by any electronic or mechanical means, including information storage and retrieval systems, without written permission from the author, except for the use of brief quotations in a book review.

This book is a work of fiction. Names, characters, places and incidents are the products of the author's imagination or used fictitiously. Any resemblance to the actual events, locales or persons, living or dead, is entirely coincidental.

Join the Sparks Fly Romance VIP list for free by visiting this link: https://sparksflyromance.com/bronson5/

Cover illustration and design, Edie Murphy.

Editors, Edie Murphy and Robb Fulcher

02.23.23

To Edie
The book wouldn't be as good without you.

1

TYLER

Driving from Santa Monica to Hollywood on a Friday night didn't help my already cranky mood. I wanted to go home and be with my kids, but our user experience ratings had plummeted in the last quarter--especially in relation to our "mingles."

The lifeblood of eMingle, the app that had made me rich, rested in our live events for singles. I needed to find out what the hell was going on.

The SUV in front of me swerved, almost side-swiping a parked Tesla, and then it slowed to ten miles below the speed limit.

I fought the urge to blare my horn and give them the finger. Nope, gonna be cool. I changed lanes, peering into the driver's seat as I passed to see the precise flavor of moron I'd been driving behind.

But I didn't find a moron.

Instead, I spotted a harried woman screaming into the rear-view mirror at her tantrum-ing toddler in the back seat while another older kid cried in the passenger seat. A fellow parent. Got it.

My raged quelled. I felt like an asshole. Thank God, I hadn't let my temper show. I used to be such a laid-back guy, but ever since my company expanded so fast, I seemed eternally stressed.

And, although I'd never admit it to anyone, suddenly becoming a father of two had added a layer of stress.

My therapist told me it was a lot to handle at once, but I hated admitting anything negative concerning my children. My mother always blamed me for "destroying her youth," and I vowed my kids would never feel like a burden. They'd gotten enough rejection from their mom abandoning them.

I'd already missed the start of their lives because I didn't know they existed. Thinking about missing out, I remembered I was going to miss bedtime tonight. My heart ached. I hated missing bedtime.

"Siri, call Milda," I said. I needed to hear their voices and say goodnight.

"Hello, Mr. Tyler," Milda, my new nanny, answered. My uncle, William Bronson, was the only one in our family called Mr. Bronson. The rest of us were called by our first names.

I didn't require the "mister," but Milda seemed to prefer it even though I'd been telling her it wasn't necessary for the two weeks she'd been with us.

"I'm getting ready to head into my work function, and I just wanted to say hello to the kids."

"What time do you expect to be home?" she asked.

I took a breath to calm myself. We'd discussed it twice before. "Midnight. But I'll try to make it sooner."

"Very good, Mr. Tyler," she said, and then I heard her call the children.

"Hey Dad!" Riley, my daughter, said as she picked up the telephone.

My heart danced. It'd taken a while since her foster placement for her to call me "dad." But in the last couple of months, after she realized I'd started the paperwork for her adoption, she'd started saying it regularly.

"Hey Riley-roo, what are you up to?"

"Miss Milda won't let us have waffles."

"We can have waffles tomorrow, but promise me, you'll at least taste everything on your plate at dinner? Remember, you approved the menu."

"It's hard to know what you're going to be hungry for in advance."

"Tomorrow we'll freestyle the whole day, but we still have to eat our vegetables, okay?"

"Fine," she said.

"Me! My turn!" Renzo screamed in the background.

"Ren wants to talk to you," Riley said.

"Okay. Love you, sweetie. I'll be home late, so don't stay up. Okay?"

"Okay."

"Daddy!" Renzo screamed into the phone.

"Hey kiddo! Are you being a good boy?"

"Guess what?" he said.

I knew what was coming. His sister had taught him this.

"What?" I asked.

"Kitten butt," he said, screaming with laughter.

"It's chicken butt!" Riley corrected in the background.

"Chitten butt," Renzo said. He was still having trouble pronouncing his words.

His development was delayed, but he had a speech therapist. Both the kids had multiple therapists. Their addict mom, my ex, had done a real number on them. Me, too.

"Mr. Tyler," Milda said, returning to the call. "I don't appreciate you riling up the children this close to bedtime."

"I'm sorry, Milda. It wasn't deliberate."

If Milda worked at my company, she wouldn't have dared to talk to me like that, but finding an experienced nanny had proven to be even harder than finding good coders. It didn't help that my kids were a handful.

"Don't forget to be home by midnight, and, also, I won't be here over the weekend as per our agreement."

"I haven't forgotten." The woman reminded me of things as if I were one of my kids. I chalked it up to an occupational hazard.

"Very good," she said.

We said our goodbyes as I turned onto Hollywood Boulevard. I opted to drive past the Roosevelt Hotel and looked for a spot on the street, so I could avoid the long line waiting for the valet after the event ended.

I wanted to salvage the night by hitting the gym before going home. My new house had a great gym, but it was downstairs near Milda's room. We'd sound-proofed the room, but I lift super heavy, so the weights hitting the mat, and the plates clanking, made too much noise.

I turned off of Orange Drive and onto Hawthorne Avenue. I realized the stupid Honda in front of me had stopped in the middle of the street, and now her reverse lights were on. What the fuck?

I honked my horn and shot her the bird. So much for being patient.

The oblivious driver in the Honda looked in her rear-view mirror and waved hello to me. I scoffed and shook my head. If she didn't have the sense to know when she was being flipped off, I didn't have to feel guilty about losing my temper. What fun it must be to be so oblivious! Just Mr. Magoo-ing her way through life, leaving the rest of us in her wake.

My cell rang. I hit the button on my steering wheel and answered it.

"Where are you?" Meredith asked without even saying hello. I loved my sister, but she could be demanding.

"What's gone wrong now?" I asked, monitoring the Honda, continuing to inch in reverse. How far back was she going to go?

I honked. Miss Oblivious waved back at me again.

For crying out loud! I'm not saying hello, I'm saying don't back into me, you idiot!

"Nothing's wrong exactly," Meredith said. "The news crew might be late, but I think she's going with the single billionaire uses his singles app angle."

"Damn it. It's bad enough I let you guys talk me into participating tonight. You know I'm doing this just to experience the event for myself."

"You could actually meet someone, and I think you need it. You're getting way too cranky," she said.

The damn Honda was still backing up. She was going to back right into me! I honked my horn as I checked my rear-view mirror and put my car into reverse. "What the fuck is wrong with you?"

"What the fuck is wrong with you?" my sister shot back.

"No, I was talking to this moron in front of me," I said.

The Honda performed a two-point turn by reversing into a driveway. It was actually an impressive maneuver, except for the part where she'd almost backed into me.

The driver pulled alongside me, rolled down her window, and stopped.

I looked over at her, but didn't roll down my window. She had long, dark brown hair that had a slight wave to it. She smiled and motioned at me to roll down my window as if I wasn't ignoring her.

It was obvious she would not go away, so I rolled down my window.

"Hey, thanks for backing up for me," she said, her smile beaming.

"I didn't have a choice," I replied.

She laughed. Her grey-ish green eyes squinted as she did. "Well, thanks anyway."

Her voice wasn't high-pitched like I'd imagined it to be. She sounded confident and casual. You wouldn't know she drove like an idiot by the way she talked.

"If you're looking for parking," she continued, "there's two spots right over there. It's free after six!"

"Yeah," I said. "I was just looking for a place to turn around."

"Uh-oh! There's a car coming. I'll save your spot," she said.

I wanted to tell her not to bother, but she sped away. Sure, now she could drive fast. I rolled my eyes and made a U-turn.

"Who was that?" Meredith asked. I'd almost forgotten I was on the phone.

"Just someone who can't drive."

"How long until you're here?"

"Five minutes. I'm snagging a spot on the street."

"We're not broke anymore. You can afford to valet."

"The valet gets swamped when our event is over, and I hate standing there waiting with all of our users."

"God forbid, you actually mingle when you own a company called eMingle," Meredith said.

The brunette had pulled her car up to the curb in a way that took up both spots.

I honked, she waved, and then pulled back, giving

me the space to park in front of her. Saving the spot wasn't necessary, but I appreciated her thoughtfulness--no matter how hair-brained it was.

"Meet me on The Bridge," Meredith said. The Bridge was the room that overlooked the Tropicana Pool and Bar, where we held our mingles.

"Will do."

I hung up as I watched in my rearview mirror the brunette getting out of her vehicle. My gaze drifted from her wavy dark brown hair to her body. Damn.

She was wearing a light colored dress with pink flowers on it. It had one of those scoop necks with thin straps that went over her toned shoulders. It showed off her tits without being too showy. I hadn't expected her to be that hot. No wonder she assumed I'd be happy to talk to her. Any man would be.

She bent down to get something out of her back seat.

I couldn't help but look at her ass. The dress was short, but not too short. Although, with her bending over like that, I got a great view of her legs.

My car jolted as I heard a thud. Her car alarm went off.

What the?

I looked up to see who the fuck had just run into my car. That's when I realized. I was still in reverse, and my foot had slipped from the brake. Who was the idiot now? Fuck!

2

BETTY

I closed my eyes as the pain stabbed at the back of my head from hitting the top of my car door frame. Holding my head and stumbling a little, I stood up. The impatient dude in the SUV Porsche had backed into my old Honda. Seriously?

That's why I always back up slowly.

I steadied myself by holding the top of my car. Please let my car and my head be okay. The last thing I needed was bills. As it was, it looked like I might need to stay at my temporary housing for another month.

"Are you okay?"

"You backed into me, and I hit my head," I mumbled. I looked up to find the driver of the other car standing in front of me. A look of concern had replaced his formerly irritated expression.

Whoa! I hadn't realized how big this guy was in his car. He was all shoulders, chest, and muscle.

"I know. I'm sorry. It's all my fault."

The initial sting of pain faded, and I realized I hadn't hit my head too hard. Well, at least I hoped. Sometimes my bright-side thinking causes me to think things are fine when they're not. Was that this time?

"We'll exchange insurance information in two seconds," he said. "I don't think there's any damage, but you never know."

He whipped out his phone and started taking pictures of our cars. Is that what you do? I'd never gotten into an accident before.

I grabbed my purse out of the backseat and dug past the kids' toys and fruit rolls to get my phone. Taking his lead, I took a few photos, even though I did not know what I was taking a picture of.

"Your bumper has some scratches. I'll make sure it's taken care of," he said, pointing to a few scrapes in the middle.

I looked closer. "Oh that! That's from when I let my friend borrow my car. That was there already."

He looked over at me. "Most people would've tried to get me to pay for that."

I laughed. "I doubt that."

He shook his head as if he didn't believe me. "How's your head?"

I reached up and put my hand in my hair. "Is there a bump?"

He stepped closer, his muscular chest inches from me. I breathed in the woody scent of his aftershave.

"I don't see anything," he said. "Where did you hit it?"

I parted my hair and pointed at the spot on my head. His hands brushed mine as he gently felt for a bump. A zing of electricity whipped through me.

"It's a little red," he said, his deep voice soft and rumbly. "Do you need me to take you to urgent care or call an ambulance, to be safe?"

"No!" I said, stepping back. The idea of getting into an ambulance and paying a fortune for a bump on the head scared the crap out of me.

Judging from his startled expression, I realized I caught him off guard. "There's no point in doing something so drastic for just a bump on the head."

He nodded. "Okay, if something comes up, you can contact my insurance company, and they'll work it out."

He went back to his car to get his paperwork. I guess I was supposed to do the same?

I dug into my glove box and found my insurance stuff underneath some kids' toys. When I got up, he was standing there. Had he been checking out my ass just now?

I felt flattered. It had to be my new dress. That boded well for tonight.

I handed him my insurance info. He took a picture, so I did the same with his paperwork. I looked up at him as I handed back his insurance card. Damn, he was handsome. I rarely liked super muscle-bound guys, but there was something about the kindness in his brown eyes that softened the hard angles of his face and body.

"So if you're sure everything is okay, I'll be going

then," he said, his former impatient demeanor returning.

"Okay, then."

"Thanks for your honesty and understanding," he said, handing me back my insurance card.

"Of course," I said, but he'd already turned his back on me. His car beeped as he set the alarm and took off down the street.

Okay, Mr. Grumpy. You have a great night, too.

I exhaled, grabbed my oversized purse, locked my car, and checked my app for the nearest coffee shop. My phone dinged with a text.

It was from Caitlyn, my old boss: *Don't chicken out. Remember, you're the one doing the picking.*

I smiled as I texted back: *Got here early. I'm going to grab a coffee beforehand. Thanks again for gifting me the dating app membership and the dress.*

Caitlyn texted me back: *I knew you'd never go if I didn't push you. Focus on having fun!*

I texted her back: *I'll try. Say hello to Aubrey for me.*

She hearted my comment, and I put my phone into my pocket. I missed them, and I worried that I'd made the wrong call by staying in Los Angeles instead of moving with them to Atlanta.

But tonight would not be a night of regrets. I had my first designer dress on, my strapless adhesive push-up bra on tight, and the night off. Tonight I was going to cut loose and have a great time.

3

TYLER

I hit the Mezzanine button on the elevator and headed to The Bridge. All I wanted to do was put that embarrassing scene with the brunette behind me and find out what was going wrong at these events.

Maybe Meredith was right. Maybe I should try to meet someone. I sighed. There was no way I could entertain a relationship right now.

I was bad at relationships before I had zero spare time. I'd be even worse at them now.

I stepped off the elevator and made my way to the bridge. My sister spotted me and came right over.

She handed me an iPhone. "Use this for your matches. I've got your profile all set up. The news crew is going to go live after the event, so you'll have to stick around."

"Damn, I was hoping to get to the gym."

"You can go after."

I didn't bother telling my sister that I needed to get back home for the nanny. We went through some of the last-minute changes for tonight's event, and then it was time for me to head to the Tropicana Pool Bar downstairs.

I had just enough time to grab a vodka soda before the event started. Our new event emcee, Christy, welcomed everyone and then rolled into a cute song on her guitar.

Starting things off with a funny song got everyone's attention and seemed like a good icebreaker.

After the song, she warmed up the attendees with five minutes of standup about dieting and life in Los Angeles. Between the comedy and the drink, I was feeling much better.

The attendees seemed to respond well to her, and I made a note to read over the user surveys to see what they thought of her. I hoped her hosting added a much-needed feminine touch to our events, which had gotten a reputation online as getting a bit "bro-ey" meaning that player dudes who wanted to hookup had infiltrated our site.

"Okay, minglers," Christy said, after her last joke got an applause break. "It's time for the main event. Here's how it's going to work."

As she spoke, a screen came down with a video to help with the demonstration. Two actors appeared on screen as a couple of users. We'd recently filmed this and added a few additional features to the events to increase the feeling of safety and to make any creepers feel less welcome.

"So first off, you all need to open your app and hit the mingle button. You'll know you've done it when the confetti screen appears and the horns play."

People hit their apps. I almost forgot to hit mine. The room was a sea of horns playing the "dunna nunt nuh-nah" sound that the word "charge" usually followed.

People laughed, and the host continued. "When the bell up there sounds, a number will pop up on your screen. Go to that station and meet your first match. A conversation starter will appear on the screen if you need it. If you don't like that one, you can hit the green button and get another.

"You'll get to talk to your matches for twenty minutes. During that time, you can opt to hit the "overtime" button, and if your partner does the same, you'll remain where you are and spend the next session with them. But don't worry, you can do it on the sly, so you don't have to be embarrassed."

The screen showed an actress pointing exaggeratedly in another direction. Her match looked in that direction, and she hit the button as she winked at the camera.

"Don't worry if things get awkward. Our staff of Merry Minglers," she said, pointing to someone wearing a red T-shirt, "will pop into conversations to make sure you're having a good time."

The screen showed the actors staring off into space

and a guy in a red shirt coming by and starting a conversation. The host continued. "But, if for any reason, you're not feeling like you can stay for the full twenty minutes, you can hit the escape hatch button, and one of our Merry Minglers will discreetly come by to rescue you," she said.

On screen, the actress hits her button and a staffer in a red shirt pops into the frame with a hook and drags her match away.

Everyone laughed.

The vibration of my personal cellphone buzzed against my chest. I'd set it to do not disturb. The only numbers that would go through were my sister's and my nanny's cells. My heart pounded as I reached into the inside pocket of my jacket.

Milda's name popped up on my caller ID. She wouldn't call unless it was urgent.

"What's happened?" I asked, getting straight to the point. I rushed to a private corner so I could speak more freely.

"I can't take it anymore. I quit!" she said.

Not again! "Please, just stay through the night, and we can work something out in the morning."

"They've locked me out of the house. I'm lucky I had my phone with me."

"You mean they're in the house alone?" I asked.

"Yes, and I don't have my keys to get back in. You need to come home right away. I can see them in the kitchen, and I think nothing good is going to come of that."

They were alone in the house, and my place in Malibu was an hour away!

4

BETTY

Since it was an open bar, I decided I'd allow myself one cocktail to loosen up, and it was working. The tension from the car weirdness had faded, and I'd committed myself to being relaxed and having a good time.

I would not worry about "winning over" anyone. No more Miss Nice Gal. It was one thing to see the best in people. It was a whole other thing to settle for someone who didn't treat me right. And I wouldn't do that again.

Knowing there was an escape hatch relaxed me, even though I knew I could never push that button. It would humiliate whoever I was with, and I'd hate to embarrass anyone.

The host ran through a few more details, and then she announced, "let's get ready to mingle!" using the same cadence as that boxing announcer. Everyone laughed, and I looked at my app to find out what "station" to go to first.

A cartoon cupid shot an arrow out of his bow, and it hit a target that was seventeen. Then, a face and name popped up on my screen--Tyler B.

The face looked familiar. Had I seen him on a show or in a fitness ad or something?

I worried he was way too good looking for me. I'd never been insecure about my looks until I moved to Los Angeles. It felt like everyone here was a model, and I was a troll crawling out from under a bridge.

I looked for station seventeen, but the stations near me were in the fifties and thirties. I hunted for a few minutes. My anxiety grew. I hated being late. Tardiness was the height of disrespect.

I spotted a woman in a red shirt. Her name tag said Meredith. "Excuse me, Meredith?"

She stopped and raised her eyebrows. "How can I help?"

"I am supposed to meet a Tyler at station seventeen, but I don't know where that is."

"Tyler? Let me see," she said, glancing over at my screen. She hooked her arm around mine and sped me across the patio. "Is this your first mingle with us?"

"Very first. I'm kind of nervous. My membership was a going-away gift from my old boss."

"What you do for a living?" Meredith asked.

"I'm a nanny, but I'm in between gigs."

She stopped and stared at me. "That's so perfect! I

have a feeling you're gonna have a fantastic time tonight."

We weaved through the tabletops and over to a set of chaise lounges by the pool. It looked like I had one of the better stations for my very first meet up. Although the chaise across from mine was empty.

"I guess I wasn't the only one having trouble finding this station," I said, taking a seat and plopping my giant-ass purse down next to me.

The gong on the app bonged, which showed the start of the first "mini mingle."

The conversation starter button popped up on my screen, along with the escape hatch button.

"Don't worry, I'll find him," Meredith said. "He's probably lost."

"Here!" she said, stopping a waiter and commandeering hors d'oeuvres off his tray.

"Those are for--" he started, but then he stopped. "I'll go back and get more. Did you need anything else?"

Meredith turned to me as if to ask me if I needed anything more.

I shook my head no.

She put the tray in front of me. "Don't worry. These are on the house. Promise me you'll stay right here."

I nodded yes and forced myself not to feel guilty for commandeering someone else's snacks. They looked good. Stuffed mushrooms and what looked like fried wontons. I tasted one of each. So good!

I glanced around the patio. I loved the decor. Everything about the Roosevelt exuded a classic Hollywood vibe.

Palm trees surrounded the enormous rectangular pool. Since it was half past seven, the sun had come down, and the pool was well lit, showing off the David Hockney painted pattern on the bottom.

As the sun faded, the air chilled. I wondered if I shouldn't have left my sweater in the car. But it'd seemed a shame to cover up the dress.

Looking around, it seemed like everyone was having fun. The longer I waited, the more nervous I got. Was my mini-date avoiding me because he didn't like my picture?

Who was this Tyler B, anyway? I opened my app and looked at the photo. He was handsome, but now that he was late, my mind interpreted his smile as arrogant.

I know where I recognized that face. It was Mr. Grumpy from the street! His profile photo was just his face, but when I swiped through his other pics, I saw those broad shoulders.

First, he backs into my car, and then he's late for a twenty-minute date when I know he got here over an hour ago. What a jerk!

I grabbed my phone, and I was just about to hit the escape hatch when another Merry Mingler stopped at my station.

"What are you doing sitting alone?" he asked, his voice loud.

Everyone turned and stared. My face reddened with embarrassment. Total humiliation.

5

TYLER

Nothing about tonight was going right, and it just got even worse. I needed to get my kids to unlock the damn door. I called the house phone.

Thank goodness, my eldest, Riley, picked up the phone.

"Hello," she said, as if nothing was happening.

"Open that door right this minute, young lady!" I growled into the phone.

"Daddy, she's mean to us," Riley whined.

"How? How was she mean? And keep in mind I have cameras in the house."

Riley had made up that the bruise she'd gotten on her arm was from our last nanny. I'd gone ballistic when she told me, but it turned out Riley had lied. Her therapist said she was acting out because she was testing to see if I would give her away like her mother had.

My heart ached for Riley, but I wouldn't let her make false accusations.

"She's doesn't listen to anything I say," Riley said. "And Renzo says she smells."

Renzo yelled into the phone. "She smells like oily water!"

"Oily water?" I asked.

Someone poked me in the arm, hard. I knew it had to be Meredith. Nobody else would dare.

"He means barley water," Meredith said. "It's from Mary Poppins."

I rolled my eyes.

"Your date is waiting. She's the only one sitting out there alone."

"My kids locked the nanny out of the house," I said.

Meredith laughed. "Those kids are little monsters."

"It's not funny, she's quit, and Malibu, it's like an hour from here."

"Get them to let her back in, and I'll call Nick's dad and see if he's nearby," Meredith said, stepping away to give me space. Nick is Meredith's husband, and my best friend from high school. We reconnected when he became the angel investor for this app.

"Open that door right this minute, Riley, or I'm taking away all of your devices for the entire week, and you can say goodbye to Legoland next week as well."

"Dad!" Riley screamed. "I'm just gonna make pancakes. Then I'll let her in."

"Don't you dare turn on anything in that kitchen!"

She hung up the phone. I dialed it again.

"Hi Daddy!" Renzo answered, obviously amped up on sugar. They'd probably raided the candy jar. I'm gonna have to buy a jar with a lock on it when I get home.

"Hey son," I said, keeping my voice friendly. "I need you to go over to the sliding glass door and open it for me. Can you do that for me, champ?"

"Okay, Daddy!" he said, running to the door.

"Don't!" I heard Riley yell in the background.

The phone thudded to the ground, but I could've sworn I heard the door slide open before the call disconnected.

Meredith approached me. "Nick's dad will be there in fifteen minutes."

My call waiting beeped. It was Milda. I clicked over. "Are you inside?"

"Yes, and I am going to send them to their rooms while I pack my bags."

"Their Uncle M will be there in fifteen minutes. Can you put the kids on?"

"I will not hand them my telephone," she said to me. I heard her yell to the children. "Your Uncle M will be here in fifteen minutes. Go to your rooms."

"I'll take it from here," Meredith said.

Meredith dialed. "Hi Riley, It's Aunt Meredith!"

It didn't feel right to just leave and go on with the date. I felt like I needed to go home.

"Your dad will be home after work, but your Uncle M will be there in a few minutes. Will you go to your room in the meantime as a favor for me?"

She paused. "Tell your dad you'll be good and wait."

Meredith held the phone to my ear. "I'm sorry, Daddy. I'll be good and wait until Uncle M gets here."

I exhaled. "We'll talk about this later, young lady."

Meredith took her phone back. "Just go. I don't want you to be the reason we get low feedback scores on the app. You're supposed to be solving problems, not causing them."

I opened my app to figure out where to go.

Meredith tapped me hard on the shoulder. "Station seventeen right now. It's in the back corner near the pool. Hurry! The news crew will be here any minute. "

I dashed back to the bar and looked around the pool. It was easy to find station seventeen. It was the only station with just one person there. Thank goodness one of our minglers was there talking to her. I rushed through the tables of laughing couples and over to the empty chaise lounge, accidentally hitting it with my shin. The chaise scraped the floor and nearly fell in the pool.

"Oops," I said, catching the chaise before the leg went over the edge.

"Are you okay?" she asked.

I turned, and our eyes locked. It was the brunette that I'd backed into, and now I was late and knocking shit over. Great. Just great.

6

BETTY

Why hadn't I hit the escape hatch button? That well-meaning but loud mingler had distracted me, and now it was too late.

"Glad you made it, boss," the mingler dude said and then he split.

"I think we met earlier outside. I'm Betty," I said, holding out my hand.

He gave my hand a polite shake. His hand was powerful, but he made sure not to squeeze too tight. The mixture of his tenderness and strength sent a jolt of excitement through me, but then I remembered his personality.

"Sorry for keeping you waiting," he said. "I had an emergency."

"Did you accidentally back into someone else?" I joked, but my nerves made it come out weird.

"Just a problem at home. I think it's settled now," he said, his jaw clenched tight.

"That's good."

Silence.

I glanced down at my phone. Eleven minutes. Maybe it was good that he was late.

"So what do you do for a living?" he asked.

"I'm a nanny."

He glanced down at the ground and shook his head. "Of course."

"I'm not sure how to take that," I said, trying to keep the conversation light despite not appreciating the tone of his voice.

"I'm sorry. My emergency was a problem with the nanny. She up and quit on me."

"I'm sorry that happened to you. Do you need to go home?"

"No, a family friend lives nearby. He's going to take care of them. You nannies really get your pick of families, though. It's like I work for her."

"It's hard to find a good fit," I said, trying to keep things light.

"That's putting it mildly," he mumbled.

Another silence descended on our conversation, but this one felt more hostile.

I glanced down at my phone to check the time again.

Nine minutes left! It felt like I'd been sitting here for ages.

I picked up my phone and tapped the button for the conversation starter. The escape hatch button was right next to it. That escape hatch button tempted me big time.

"So, if you had to choose between having the power of flight or the power of invisibility, which would you choose?" I asked, reading off the question.

"Is that one of the app's questions?" he asked, his face frowning.

"Yup."

He shook his head, but didn't answer.

I don't know what came over me, but my finger hit the escape button. Once I realized what I did, my heart beat in my throat as I waited to see what would happen.

7

TYLER

I racked my brain for something to say to turn this date around. I was so rusty with women.

Think, Tyler, think.

Kevin, one of our minglers came by and stopped at our station. Wow! Did we look that awkward that one of our minglers was going to have to save our date?

"Betty, I hate to interrupt," Kevin said. "The valet says there's a problem with your car in the lot. Would you mind helping us with it?"

Kevin turned to me. "Excuse us, boss."

Betty turned to me with a polite smile. "It was nice seeing you again."

Wait! She hadn't used the valet! We both parked on the street. I realized what was going on.

"Did you just escape hatch me?" I asked.

A guilty expression swept across her face.

She did escape hatch me!

She stood up and reached for her purse. "You seemed distracted by your emergency. I figured you could use the time to call home."

I stood up to say goodbye and apologized for being such an ass.

The sound of a chaise lounge scraping against the patio again nabbed my attention.

Her purse had somehow gotten stuck on the chair. She pulled at it, and it hit her in the shin. She winced and doubled over.

"Step back. Let me help," I said, noticing the purse strap was caught on the arm of the lounge.

"It's OK, I think I've got it." She pulled her purse some more to free it.

"It's the strap," I said, stepping closer.

She stepped back to give me room. I saw her heel hit the apron of the pool, and then she was losing her balance.

I reached for her and grabbed her wrist as she fell back. But she was still holding onto her purse, which made the chaise lounge lift off the patio. I felt the hard thwack of the arm of the chair bonk me on the side of my head.

Betty yelped.

A micro-second of disbelief shot through my mind. We couldn't be falling into the--

The sound of Betty splashing into the pool followed by the shock of cold water surrounding me as I plunged in right on top of her. The chaise lounge tumbled onto my back, trapping us both underneath it.

Betty flailed to get out from under me. I reached up with one hand, grabbed the stupid lounge chair, and tossed it to the other side of the pool. Then, I wrapped my arms around Betty's waist and pulled us both above water.

She coughed as I flipped her on her back and swam us toward the steps to the pool. As we got to the steps, I looked up and saw the reporter and her news crew filming us. God no!

8

BETTY

My throat burned as I coughed up chlorine water. The terror of my fall faded and embarrassment bloomed in its place.

"Don't worry, I've got you," Tyler whispered in my ear. His thick, muscular arm wrapped around my chest as he held me above the water. I floated on my back and tried to catch my breath.

In my periphery, I spotted a couple people pointing and laughing, and some woman holding up her phone to film the spectacle. A crowd of people had gathered around the pool to see what'd happened.

I avoided eye contact and stared up at one of the palm trees. The conversation starter about super powers flashed into my mind. I'd definitely choose invisibility.

Tyler guided me to the steps of the pool.

"Can you stand?' he asked.

I put my foot on the step and slipped. One of my shoes was missing.

Tyler caught me. Thank God. Something floated by my leg. I jumped and looked down. It was my not-all-that-sticky, adhesive strapless bra, just floating there next to a box of condoms. I tried to snatch it up in my hand, but it was too slippery, and floated away.

That's when I looked back at the rest of the pool. When I fell, the entire contents of my giant purse spilled out and now all my crap was scattered along the bottom of the pool.

This couldn't get any worse.

"Let's get you somewhere warm," Tyler said, picking me up and carrying me out of the pool. I realized I was shivering.

A woman's voice cut through the sound of the murmuring crowd. "So, Tyler Bronson, would you say you two fell head over heels for each other?"

I looked up, and I saw the reporter from KTLA's local news!

I buried my face in Tyler's neck and then whispered to him, "Please, get me away from everyone."

I choked on the last two words. Tears threatened. I liked to make the best of things typically, but this was the worst.

9

TYLER

I heard her sniffling as she buried her face in my chest. Had I just made her cry?

The reporter pestered me, and I wanted to just tell her to fuck off. What had she asked? Did we fall head over heels for each other?

I forced a smile. "I definitely fell for her, but I'm pretty sure she thinks I'm all wet. You're going to have to excuse us."

Meredith rushed over, accompanied by a security guard. I shot her a look. She knew it meant to get these people the hell away from me.

She whispered to the security guard. He cleared the path for us while Meredith jumped in front of the reporter and cameraman, blocking them from following us.

"That's our eMingle founder. He likes to make a splash."

I didn't stick around and took the backstairs to The

Bridge. The moment we entered, some of my staff looked up at us, horrified.

"Out! Now! And get some dry clothes and towels!" I ordered.

They scurried away as I sat her down on the sofa.

"No, I'll get it wet and ruin it," she said.

"I'll take care of it," I said, leaning down in front of her. "Are you okay?"

She looked away and wiped her face. Yup, she tried to fight it, but silent tears escaped out of the corner of her eyes.

One of the event workers rushed in with two large towels.

I took the towels. "We need dry clothes."

"I'm not sure--"

I glared at him. He stopped mid-sentence, nodded in agreement, and rushed out of the room.

I turned back to Betty. Her body shivered. She seemed out of it.

I draped the towel around her shoulders and noticed one dress strap had fallen. Gently, I pushed the strap back up. My fingers brushed her soft skin.

She looked up at me. I melted. Up close, she was even more beautiful.

I stared into her green eyes. "We'll get you dry and taken care of, okay?"

She nodded her head. "Okay." Her voice was soft, breathy and vulnerable--so different from the cheerful voice I'd heard earlier.

She took hold of the towel and dried her hair and then gasped as if remembering something.

"What's wrong?"

"My phone! My car keys, all my stuff! It's all at the bottom of the pool."

The high sound of her voice told me she'd reached her limit. She'd have a total breakdown if I didn't act fast.

I put my hands on each of her shoulders and looked her in the eye. "Don't worry, not for a moment. I'm on it right now. Okay?"

She nodded yes, and I dashed to the door as I grabbed my phone. But the damn thing had powered down.

"Hey!" I shouted to the nearest security guard. "Tell someone to guard her stuff. It's in the pool. And get someone from maintenance to fish it out. And make sure everything is here. Bring it back, pronto."

I rushed back to Betty and kneeled in front of her. "I've got everyone on it. Don't worry about a thing. I'll make sure we pay for your dress, recover your stuff, and get you home safely. We'll look over all your things before you leave and make sure nothing's missing."

She nodded and gave me a weak smile. She was being such a good sport about this. Anyone else would yell and scream their head off.

It made me feel even more guilty. "I'm so sorry about today."

"Thanks, Tyler. I don't know how this happened.

Somehow I just lost my footing, and then I dragged you in with me. I'm so sorry."

I sighed, knowing I was the one who caused her to step back, and if I hadn't been such a jackass on the date, she wouldn't have been in such a rush to get away from me.

"This is all my fault. And I don't mind being wet."

She motioned to my phone in my hand. "I hope it turns on. They're supposed to be waterproofed to a certain number of feet. I bought one of those military-grade cases for mine. Do those cases really work? Do you think maybe it survived?"

"Absolutely, and if it didn't, I'll make sure you get a new phone."

I tried to power on my phone, but it was still too waterlogged.

"They say putting it in rice helps," she said.

"You're something else."

"Was that a compliment?"

I laughed. "It was an attempt at one. I guess I'm out of practice giving them."

She chuckled along. "Practice it more. It's a good time."

"If you say so." I peeled off my jacket, and I thought I caught her gaze drift to my chest. I acted cool, but I took my time with my jacket just in case.

"Do you want to have a seat? Or maybe dry yourself off?" she asked, handing me a towel.

I took the towel and unbuttoned my shirt. "Thanks."

Her eyes darted back to my chest again. Yeah, she

was definitely checking me out. It made me smile. Well then, let's see how she deals with the whole shirt off. I took my time stripping off my shirt. She averted her gaze, but when she looked back at me, her eyes widened. I could've sworn she did a double take, which tickled me even more.

People stare at me a lot because I've gotten big--too big, according to some. But Betty, looking at me, sent a thrill through me.

"Do you mind?" I asked, motioning to the small sofa.

"No, of course not. Now I won't have to feel like I'm the only one who ruined it."

I chuckled as I sat next to her and draped my shirt over the arm to dry. "I'm bigger than you, so you can say I ruined most of it."

She smiled and nodded. "You're definitely big," she said and then blushed. "I meant bigger." She gestured to me as she stopped talking.

She was flustered and I enjoyed it.

"Was that a compliment?" I joked.

She laughed and shook her head. "Nope. Just a fact."

It was good to see her laugh. She'd stopped shivering.

My thigh brushed against her skin of her leg. A felt a pang below the waist. Damn. There was something about this girl. Her sweet demeanor and her adorable face drew me to her. She was both cute and sexy. It didn't hurt that her dress was practically see-through.

I opted not to tell her because I didn't want her to

feel self-conscious, but I'd make sure no one came in here until we got her some dry clothes to wear.

It sucked that I wasn't at a better place in my life, and that I'd made such a shitty impression on her on our mini-date and when I hit her car. At another time, maybe we could've dated or something?

Nope. Forget about it, Tyler. Knowing my history, I was only attracted to her because she was in need. I had a tendency to be the rescuer type, and I'd been going to support meetings and Al-Anon meetings to get over my codependent tendencies.

I heard the door open, and I jumped up to tell whoever it was to get the fuck out.

But it was Meredith carrying a heavy garbage bag.

She set it down on the floor. "We fished your stuff out of the pool." Meredith held up a high-heeled sandal with a torn strap. "This didn't make it, though."

"How about my phone?" Betty asked, rushing over to look in the bag.

"I kept it separate," Meredith said, reaching into her pants pocket and handing it to Betty. "Somehow, it's still on."

"The case! It worked!" Betty said.

It made me happy to see her relief.

Meredith turned to me. "Tyler, we just need you outside for a moment."

I wanted to tell my sister I'd deal with it later, but I could tell by Meredith's expression whatever it was couldn't wait.

"Betty? Do you mind if I step out? It'll only be a

couple of minutes," I said, standing up and pulling back on my wet shirt.

Betty nodded as she rifled through the wet trash bag of her items. How much stuff could one person put in a purse, anyway?

I watched as she pulled out crayons and a soggy notebook.

"Is there another trash bag I can use to toss out the things that won't make it? I feel weird putting wet stuff on the carpet," Betty said.

I buttoned my shirt and nodded. "Just put them on the carpet for now, and we'll get you another bag. I'll be right back."

I stepped outside of the room with Meredith, where the hotel manager, the KTLA reporter, and a staffer holding up a phone were waiting for me.

Meredith pulled me out of earshot from the crowd and explained the situation. "The hotel wants to make sure that it's our liability, not theirs. If she sues, I have our lawyer on the phone. And the news crew wants to interview you and Betty by the pool. The cameraman is setting up the shot there now."

This shit show of a night just wouldn't stop.

10

BETTY

I went through the wet garbage bag of stuff that had been in my purse. I needed to find out what was salvageable and what wasn't. The pile of stuff that needed to be thrown away had grown into a sopping mess.

This couldn't be good for the carpet. Tyler had said he'd take care of it, so I tried not to worry too much about it. From what I could gather, he worked here and was pretty important. People at the bottom don't get to bark orders like that.

Plus, he drove what looked like a super expensive Porsche SUV. I wasn't good at gauging those kinds of things. Having grown up as a foster kid, anyone who had a house and could afford to go on a plane somewhere seemed rich to me.

My thoughts drifted to Tyler. He'd carried me all the way from the pool, up the backstairs, and into this room like it was nothing. I closed my eyes, thinking of his arms wrapped around me. Even his neck was veiny and muscular. What crunches do you do for that?

I was glad I was sitting down when he touched my shoulder to help me with my dress strap. My knees would've buckled if I'd been standing.

That man exuded masculinity, and even though I'd never been attracted to the big, protective type, I had to fight my brain from fantasizing about the idea of breaking down that rough exterior of his.

I shook my head. Wow! Caitlyn was right. I do want to fix everybody. She said it was my way of getting close, but not too close. I sighed. None of that mattered. I needed to dry off, make sure I had all my important stuff, and get home.

I rummaged through my soaked things. Thank God my car was so old that I used a metal key. I don't know if those car fobs are waterproof.

I worried that Tyler's fancy fob from his Porsche might've gotten drenched. I'd have to remind him. If he waited until he got to his car at the end of the night, it could be forever for AAA or tow truck to get there.

Nope. He could take care of himself. I stared at all this junk. It mortified me that Tyler had told people to guard a bunch of half-broken kids' toys, fruit roll-ups, and other junk. My giant ass purse had ripped almost entirely in half, rendering it useless. It'd had a tear in it for months, but my fight with that chaise lounge and the water finished it off.

I found my wallet. All my ID and credit cards were there, along with my emergency cash--fifteen dollars in singles and two bucks in change. I used to carry an emergency twenty-dollar bill, but the last thing you want in an emergency is to look for someone to make change.

I took off my one shoe and dried it off with the towel. Then, I realized the other shoe was broken, it might as well be in the throwaway pile.

The sopping wet pile of items that I needed to toss was getting pretty high. I really needed that trash bag. Maybe someone outside could get me one, or maybe there was a trashcan in the hall I could dump this stuff in.

I wrapped the towel around me and padded barefoot on the carpet to the door. Tyler's voice echoed in the hallway. He wasn't talking loud, but he was definitely pissed.

"No, we're absolutely insured for this, and I don't think she's going to sue. I'll make sure she doesn't sue," he said. "Do you really think that's necessary?"

Who was he talking to on the phone? And what did he mean I wouldn't sue? What was there to sue for?

I looked down at my dress. My boss's gift had definitely been destroyed. But I wouldn't have to sue them to replace or fix it, would I? I opened the door a crack and spied on what was happening.

Tyler was on the telephone next to Meredith plus a bunch of people I didn't know.

Meredith tapped on Tyler's shoulder while he was on the phone. "The news crew is by the pool waiting for you two," she said to him. "Wrap your call, and convince Betty to come down with you to be on the news. You'll go live in ten minutes, so make it quick."

Live in ten minutes! No! I had to get the hell out of here.

I spotted another door and rushed across the room, leaving a river of water behind me. Please don't be a closet.

I cracked open the door and took a quick look. Bingo! It led out to the hallway, and the elevator was just five yards away. I could hear Tyler talking on the phone. I dashed over to my garbage bag of stuff and grabbed it.

Damn, it was heavy. My original thought was that I'd tiptoe quietly to the elevator, but my clanging bag of bullshit made that impossible. So I opted to sprint to the elevator. The doors opened a few seconds later.

A couple with their luggage stared at me like I was the Creature from the Black Lagoon. I ignored them, hopped in the elevator, and pushed the button for the lobby. They moved to the back corner of the elevator to stay away from me.

The doors opened, and me and my garbage bag got out of the elevator.

"Excuse me, miss!" someone called out to me.

I panicked and broke into a sprint across the lobby in my bare feet, my wet bag of junk clanging against my leg in one hand, and my towel flapping in my right hand.

"Miss!" the voice called again.

I didn't look back. "Sorry, I'm in a rush! Talk to

Tyler from the eMingle thing. He'll take care of everything!"

I bolted out the door and onto Hollywood Boulevard. The second my bare feet hit the pavement, I recoiled in disgust. My brain conjured up memories of watching a dude drop a deuce on the sidewalk outside of the Hollywood Wax Museum, right across the street.

They'd parked the KTLA news van in front of the hotel. Shoot! If they needed to grab something from the truck, they'd spot me for sure.

But I couldn't bear the grimy, possibly feces-filled street on my feet. I tossed my towel onto the ground and used the towel as my shoes.

I shuffled along Hollywood Boulevard as fast as I could, dragging the towel underneath my feet with each step. The grime from Hollywood Boulevard covered the bottom. So gross.

My wet hair dripped down my back and combined with my sweat. How could I be cold and sweaty and the same time?

Tourists gaped at me as I did my sad towel skate down Hollywood Boulevard. I slid across Andy Garcia's star, narrowly avoiding a piece of gum stuck to the tip of the left point.

When I moved to Los Angeles from Las Vegas, I thought it'd be a glamorous adventure.

I was so wrong.

I reached the corner of Orange and Hollywood, and made a right. My car wasn't far now, but there weren't as many people on Orange. I was glad no one was staring at me, but I wished I'd fished my mace and keys out of the garbage bag in advance.

I got to Hawthorn and spotted my car. Thank goodness. This nightmare was over.

As I passed under a streetlight, a dude on the other side of the street yelled over at me. "Nice nips, garbage lady!"

I looked down. My dress was totally see through. You could see everything! Perfect. Just perfect.

11

TYLER

I wrapped up the call with my lawyer, and I dreaded asking Betty to sign a waiver for the stupid interview. She'd been through enough, and the way she buried her sweet little face in my neck upon spotting the news crew earlier convinced me she wouldn't want to do it.

"Just ask her," Meredith argued.

"I feel that she'd do it even if she didn't want to," I said.

"You mean the person who you used to be?" Meredith asked.

"I've recovered."

"We need our business to recover, so get in there."

What I needed to do was figure out a way to make it up to her. I vowed to get her a new dress and replace all the things in her bag. Maybe I could take her out on a proper date to make it up to her.

THE NEW SINGLE DAD BILLIONAIRE

I shook my head at my thought. Why would that make it up to her? She totally hated me.

I walked back into The Bridge. She wasn't there. There was just a pile of her soggy stuff, and a trail of wet footprints leading to the other door.

I rushed over to see if she was in the hallway or something. She shouldn't be wandering around in a see-through dress in Hollywood. What if she wasn't okay? What if she swallowed too much water? I ran out of the room and looked both ways, but she was gone.

"Tyler!" Meredith called.

"She's gone!" I yelled back to my sister.

Meredith rushed over to me and grabbed my arm. "You'll have to do the interview without her."

"She's wandering the streets of Hollywood, cold and wet."

"There's no time, Tyler. She obviously wants nothing to do with us."

"We need to find her."

"The interview goes live soon. Get down there. If we do it right, we may even get more business from it. There's a real buzz downstairs."

I knew my sister was right, but guilt stabbed at my heart. I'd wrecked that poor girl's entire evening, and there was no way I'd get to make it up to her.

* * *

LAST NIGHT'S incident hadn't been a complete disaster, at least not for business. The news story had blown up, and so far it seemed like it'd generated good publicity, but I wondered how Betty was taking it. The pained sound of her voice asking me to get her away from all the people staring at us when I carried her out of the pool made me think she wouldn't enjoy all the attention.

I dialed my sister to see if she'd had any luck getting in touch with Betty.

"Hey!" Meredith answered. "I thought weekends were for the kids."

"Their Uncle M is here, and I canceled our trip to Legoland because of their misbehaving."

"My father-in-law loves kids. I'm glad he can play with yours. Takes the pressure off me and Nick for awhile."

"Is Mick pressuring you?"

"He just says stuff like if you ever had kids you'd be a great mom. Or if you two ever had a child, I bet that kid would be great."

"Subtle," I said with a laugh and then got to the point of my call. "Any news about last night?"

"We've gone viral. It's amazing! We've had over 250,000 new users, and it's the perfect users. Women and people under thirty."

"Yeah, that's great, but I was wondering if you got in touch with Betty."

"The phone number she gave us rang into a full voicemail."

"Did she fill out a comment card?"

"No, but I know we'll reach her. Why are you so concerned?"

"Last I saw her, she was shivering in a see-through dress wearing one shoe. For all I know, she got knifed on the street by some nutcase on Hollywood Boulevard!"

"Knifed on the street!" Meredith chuckled. "It's not like you to give a damn about anyone other than your kids. The internet thinks you two are a match. And your algorithm picked her out. Maybe you should ask her out when we track her down."

"She and I are definitely not a match. And even if we were, I doubt she wants to hear from me, and I don't have time. Between the kids, eMingle, and my crazy ex, I'm drowning already. "

"Alright, alright. I've got great news, but promise me you'll treat it like great news and not be all pissy."

"Nothing about this sounds like great news."

"Since you're heading to New York to interview some new coders, we've got you booked on *Your Morning* to talk about the video."

"I have to cancel that trip and work from home. Mick is busy during the week with that dance thing, and I lost my nanny yesterday."

"No! The recruiter set up the meetings with the top coders. We already lost two to Google last week."

"There's just no way I can leave the kids."

"I'll call Nick's friend, Grace at the agency, to get you someone right away. And don't forget to tell the potential recruits about our retention bonus structure."

"That's if I can make it. I doubt the agency will find-_"

"You're going if I have to watch your kids myself.

We need those coders. Besides, Grace owns the top agency. Your kids can't be the worst kids in LA. She'll find someone."

I sighed, and then an idea struck me. "Do you think I should offer a retention bonus like I do for the coders, so I can get a nanny who will stick around?"

"Couldn't hurt. I'll tell Grace."

I sighed. "Any other news?"

"The comment cards are all very positive, even from the women. They loved you in the wet shirt. One user said it was very Darcy."

"What does that mean?" I asked.

"It's from *Pride and Prejudice*. It's a good thing."

"Well, I can't dive into the pool at every one of our damn mingles."

"I've gotten some stills of you in a wet shirt, and the memes look great."

"Don't you dare!" I growled.

"Oh, I dared. We memed you up good. And it's getting shared all over the place, brother. It's about time you dealt with the media monster. It's your turn."

Meredith had used a wedding disaster moment to garner the app some free publicity before we went public. There was no way last night's swim wasn't filmed by our attendees.

"If we didn't do it, somebody else would have," I said, knowing there was no stopping it. I was going to let that go. "But the girl, Betty, she's not in any of them, right?"

"Just the footage, but not the memes."

I exhaled. "I hope she's okay."

"Our lawyers hope she doesn't sue us, but the sign regarding consent to be filmed was posted, and it's in the TOS. So we're clear on that. But I don't think she will, do you?"

"I would, but I don't think she would." My brain conjured up an image of those green eyes and that sweet face. "At the very least, I'll make sure she gets a new dress and purse."

"Don't worry. She'll call us," Meredith said.

I sighed and tried to put Betty out of my thoughts. "Besides my pool dive, did the attendees like any of the changes we made?"

"The new host, Christy, was a hit, and we're putting together a focus group of attendees from the event coming on Monday."

Taking a deep breath, I pushed my thoughts back to my kids and my business. One mini-date and my mind had been invaded by thoughts of a woman again.

I told myself I was lucky she left, and I needed to stop thinking about her.

12

BETTY

I woke up Sunday morning and debated turning my phone back on. Footage of my unexpected swim made it to the internet. My phone flooded with messages from everyone I'd ever met, plus news stations and the eMingle people.

Maybe it would've been better if my phone had died in the pool.

The noise from the couple next door fighting and kids running up and down the hallways made me want to listen to a podcast or some music on my phone. It sucked staying in a temporary apartment, but I hoped it was only a matter of time before I received a placement with another family.

I couldn't afford another month here. Plus, my car needed new tires, and the registration was due. The next gig I got, I'd be sure to save more money. I needed an emergency fund.

I'd been relying on babysitting gigs to buy groceries.

THE NEW SINGLE DAD BILLIONAIRE

There was no way I could keep my phone off any longer.

I took a deep breath, turned it on, and went to make my coffee while it buzzed with messages.

The opening beats to the eighties song "Maniac" blared out of my phone. Caitlyn had set it as her custom ring tone when I started working for her. I loved her sense of humor.

I hit the button to the coffeemaker, put in my earbuds, and answered the call. "Hey!"

"For the record, I did text before I called, but I've been trying to reach you since last night."

"Sorry, I got overwhelmed by the phone."

"I guess a lot of people saw it then," Caitlyn said.

"How did you come across it all the way in Atlanta?" I asked.

"Someone made a TikTok about it."

"Darn," I said, wishing I could will the coffeemaker to brew faster. I needed caffeine to deal with this.

"Judging from his interview, the owner of the app seemed to really like you," Caitlyn said.

"He talked about me?" I hadn't been able to bring myself to watch the whole video, but my mind replayed him in that wet shirt kneeling in front of me. A ridiculous smile took over my face.

"He's supposed to be the next Mark Zuckerberg," Caitlyn said.

"You say that like it's a good thing."

She laughed. "Not in looks or questionable morality. Just Zuck-like in that he gots that sweet, sweet tech money."

"He's probably just trying to keep me from taking his sweet tech money, or letting our disastrous mini-date make him look bad."

"I don't know about that. The way he looked at you when he was carrying you. Total swoon!" Caitlyn said.

I remembered overhearing his phone conversation with his lawyer, and I also remembered that he'd only been nice to me after I'd fallen in the water. No, he was more like the grumpy guy on the street, who I hit the escape hatch on, than the nice guy who came out of the water with me.

I exhaled and shook my head. "You're the one who told me I'm not supposed to look at people through rose-colored glasses anymore."

"Do not throw my good advice back at me when I'm staring at a gif of a hot, wet man," Caitlyn said. "But seriously, how are you? Are you okay?"

"I am, but the beautiful dress you got me. I don't think it's gonna make it."

"They should reimburse you for that."

"He said they would, but it's just a lot to deal with."

"I find it so interesting that you can handle dozens of screaming kids at a Chuck E. Cheese without a problem, but you get overwhelmed by grown-ups."

"I'm not overwhelmed by you." I laughed. She was right, though. I loved going to places like Chuck E. Cheese, Disneyland, even the toy aisle at Target. The smell of butter cream frosting on a birthday cake made my heart dance.

"Who says I'm a grown-up? Don't let the eleven-year-old fool you. But regardless, you need to spend time with the man and get busy taking care of your own family instead of everyone else's."

"Maybe one day," I said, but deep down I knew that day would never come. The closest I'd ever come to being part of a loving family would be to work for them.

I loved people and kids in my own way, but I never truly felt close to anyone. Going from foster home to foster home with people who were indifferent at best and abusive at worst, I learned to keep my distance. Some lessons can't be unlearned.

I spoke to Aubrey about school and her new bedroom for a bit, and then Caitlyn came back on the line. I told her about my skate down Hollywood Boulevard, and it cracked her up.

My call waiting beeped. I checked my caller ID expecting it to be the dating app people or another news station, but it was actually the Herzog Agency! They were the top agency in LA, and I'd registered with them just in case. But I never expected they'd call me. They only took nannies with ten years of experience and master's degrees.

Needing to work full time, I'd barely gotten through two years of college--six years sounded impossible.

"Caitlyn, I've got to go! It's the Herzog Agency!"

"Oh my God, get it. And if you need a reference, tell them I'll be here."

I clicked over to the other line and tried to sound calm as I answered. "Bethany Abel speaking."

"Bethany! I'm so glad I caught you. It's Grace Herzog, from the Herzog Agency. I have an emergency placement. We list your status in our system as available. Is that still correct?"

"Yes!" It was the owner herself calling me!

"Glad to hear it. This placement is with one of our biggest clients, so I'm handling it myself. As you know, we typically place candidates with more experience and higher education, but there were extenuating circumstances. Would it be possible for you to interview on early morning Monday for an immediate start if you and the client suited each other?"

"Yes, it's possible," I said, not wanting to sound overeager.

"Just so you know, the placement is for two children with a single parent and there will be travel involved, possibly as soon as Monday. Would you be able to make that accommodation? Your contract provides you with additional pay for travel days. Be sure to initial the pay schedule paragraphs if you're amenable to them. "

"I'll bring a packed bag to the interview."

"Perfect. I'm going to email you the contract. This is all provisional, depending on the client's approval. You'll need to sign the standard NDA paperwork, and I need to warn you the children have behavioral issues. Nothing violent, but they have had emotional problems. There are retention bonuses at the 90-day mark, and after one full year of service. The paperwork spells out all the details."

I told her about my training with troubled children at the Casey Foster Support Center in Las Vegas, and she seemed impressed. We confirmed my email address, and I promised to send the paperwork back before my interview.

I hung up the phone, did my happy dance, and vowed to ace that interview.

* * *

THE PARKING in the building was five dollars every fifteen minutes, but I didn't want to risk even the possibility of being late. I needed this job. I'd made the rash decision to not renew my temporary apartment for the next month.

If I didn't get this, I'd be in one of those seedy motels until there was another opening in the extended stay place.

But they needed someone, and I was packed and ready. I entered the elevator, determined to nail this interview.

The paperwork they'd sent over hadn't included the client's name, but I assumed that was because they needed my NDA signed before giving me any information.

Wouldn't it be amazing if I was a nanny for a major celebrity!

I got into the elevator and took a deep breath to relax myself. Good nannies were hard to find, and I was a great one. They needed me. It was all going to be okay.

The elevator doors opened, and I headed to the East Wing of the twenty-second floor, well, what I hoped was the East Wing. I was bad at east and west, and it was the first door.

Glancing at my watch, I realized that it'd taken me longer than I thought to get from the parking lot to the offices. I was only ten minutes early, and if there was a wait at the reception area, they might think I was late.

I rushed into the spacious lobby, figuring if I had the wrong office, I could dash over to the other wing. The receptionist looked up at me and smiled.

"You actually came!" she said.

Thank God! I'm in the right place.

She got up from her desk and rushed over to me. "You weren't answering your phone or messages. We've been trying to call you all weekend."

"Grace didn't tell me to expect--"

"Don't worry about a thing. We started without you, but you can join in," she said, motioning for me to follow her.

I looked at my watch. Yeah, ten minutes early. But maybe there'd been a miscommunication. I'd definitely settle it up in the interview. The receptionist led me through the open plan part of the office into a conference room. There were eight other women sitting at the table. Was this a group interview?

Nothing about my conversation with Grace indicated there were other candidates for this position, let alone nearly a dozen!

13

TYLER

Meredith entered my office with the itinerary for my appearance on *Your Morning*. I needed to tell her I wasn't going, because my new "emergency nanny" hadn't shown up.

Traveling with the kids and a stranger didn't seem like a good idea, and I hated doing morning television.

"Okay, I've got some bullet points --"

"I'm canceling the trip, and don't nag me about you watching the kids. The last time you watched them, they ate Pop-Tarts and stayed up all night. It took an entire week for us to get back on schedule."

"You keep those kids on too tight of a leash. Not everybody enjoys a schedule like you do." Meredith said.

"You can't let kids live off of Pop-Tarts," I said.

"It was waffles--the proper kind, not the gross protein powder ones you make. And they had vegetables."

THE NEW SINGLE DAD BILLIONAIRE

"Corn doesn't count."

"Kids love corn," Meredith protested.

"Kids also love to eat dirt. It doesn't make it a good idea."

"Actually, I think it is good for their immune system --"

"Don't be a smart ass."

Reece, our receptionist, rushed in. "Can you believe she showed up?"

"Who?" I asked.

The one you fell in the pool with. She's in the focus group right now."

I stood up and rushed over to the conference room. I spotted Betty, rushing for the exit.

"Betty!" I yelled across the office. Everyone stared.

She stopped for a moment. Her jaw dropped open. She shook her head and waved me off as she dashed into the reception lobby. "There's been some kind of mixup. I have a job interview in the other wing."

Without thinking, I ran after her. She rushed into the lobby of our neighbor. What business did she have with the corporate offices of Nature Pet? They were an organic pet food company.

She rushed out of the office, her expression frazzled.

"Betty, what's wrong?" I asked.

She held up a finger, signaling for me to wait a minute as she dialed her telephone.

"Yes, this is Bethany Abel. I need to speak to Grace

Herzog. It's regarding my emergency placement. You've given me the wrong address."

"Did you say Grace Herzog?" I asked. She shushed me, but a second later she looked up with a questioning expression.

"Yes, that's my agency," she said. "I'm on hold."

"Who are you supposed to meet?" I asked, piecing together what might've happened.

"I just got the address to this place, but they didn't give me the name. They were waiting for me to sign the NDA."

She was my emergency nanny placement! What were the odds?

Judging from her expression, I think she concluded the same thing.

"You're here to meet me," I said.

Her mouth dropped open again. This whole situation was impossible!

14

BETTY

I stood there, dumbfounded, still on my call. Before I could hang up, Grace Herzog came on the line. "I hear there was a mixup finding the client?"

"I think the reception desk may have misdirected me. I don't have the name of the parent I'm meeting."

"You're meeting Tyler Bronson. I'm sorry we forgot to send it."

"Tyler Bronson from eMingle?" I clarified, looking over at Tyler.

"That's the one. Should we call to say you're running late?"

"No, I just found him."

"Great! Good luck with the interview," she said and hung up.

I debated canceling the interview for a moment, but I decided against it. I needed this job, and I would be a great nanny for his kids. No matter how awkward it may be, I was going to put my best foot forward and make it impossible for him to not hire me.

15

TYLER

Stunned, I watched Betty wrap up her call. The coincidence floored me. Sure, I'd bled through four nannies already, but there was no way that I could let her watch my kids. She seemed too young, and we already didn't get along.

Meredith rushed out into the hall.

"I think I figured out the misunderstanding," Meredith said.

I turned to my sister. "We figured it out."

Meredith nodded and then looked over at Betty. "Let's get back in the office, then."

"I don't think --" I started, but my sister cut me off.

"Betty, can you give me a moment to talk to Tyler?" Meredith interrupted. "Have Reece, our receptionist, show you to Tyler's office."

"Thank you," Betty said to Meredith and then smiled and locked eyes with me." I look forward to our interview."

Damn. She still wanted this job.

When Betty was out of earshot, Meredith glared at me. "Don't even think about not hiring her."

"You can't be serious! After she deserted us on Friday night? And the entire world thinking we should 'take the plunge' and get married! No way!"

"What happened on Friday wasn't her fault. You can't opt to not hire her for that! It's bad enough she's all over the internet. And don't forget, our lawyer wants her to wave liability."

"So you think I should hire her to avoid a lawsuit? This isn't some consolation prize. These are my kids."

"She's signed with the best agency. You haven't even interviewed her! All I'm saying is that you need to be fair. None of this is her fault."

I took a deep breath. My sister was right. I couldn't reject her just because I felt awkward about what happened.

"Okay, I'll interview her."

"And now you can do the morning talk show and check out those coders in New York," Meredith said.

"Don't get ahead of yourself. I don't think we'll get along at all."

"Who cares? She'll be working when you're away from home. Hire her for the New York trip. It's not like she's gonna stick around. You lose every freaking nanny you have. This way, you ask her to settle old business. You give her the job. And everything is fine."

My sister had a point. What were the odds she'd last more than this trip? The kids were hard enough to handle at home. "I'll only hire her if she's a good nanny."

Meredith rolled her eyes. "That's all I was trying to say."

I doubted I'd actually hire Betty, but I resolved to keep an open mind in the interview. She deserved a fair shot.

16

BETTY

I willed my nerves to quiet as I waited in Tyler Bronson's office. They were probably talking about me in the hallway. Did I even really want to work for this guy? I realized it wasn't a matter of want. I needed this job.

This would probably be the only interview that Grace Herzog would send me out on. When I turned in my application, they told me it was unlikely that I would get called without having a bachelor's degree. Most of their nannies had master's degrees.

The pay for this gig was so much more than I'd ever gotten before, and if I could get that bonus, I'd actually have the beginnings of an emergency fund. Every financial expert said you need an emergency fund-- especially for someone like me with no family or even close friends.

The four hundred dollars I had in the bank, didn't cut it. I resolved to get this job and keep it for at least three months, no matter how grumpy Mr. Shoulders got.

A picture of his kids on the desk caught my attention. They looked cute.

The boy was a spitting image of his dad. He had light brown hair and blue eyes. The girl must take after her mother. She had dark brown hair, brown eyes, and a deep tan.

Finally, Tyler entered his office. I stood up.

"I'm sorry to keep you waiting. As you know, we are doing a focus group, and my sister wanted to tell me more about it."

I held my hand out for him to shake, but it took him a moment to realize that my hand was out.

"Sorry," he said. "There's so much going on."

Did I make him nervous? The idea of it made me smile.

We shook hands, and the warmth of his powerful hands reminded me of what he looked like drying off after our dip in the pool. So sexy.

"What's so funny?" he asked, taking a seat and motioning for me to sit down as well. His mouth was a straight line, and he squinted his eyes as he looked at me.

Was he trying to intimidate me? Hello dude, I've seen you with your shirt off.

Reece came in and handed him some papers. I realized it was my resume and letters of recommendation. He took his time examining them.

Seriously? Was he just going to pretend what

happened hadn't happened? I knew better than to let things go unsaid. If he was sweeping the awkwardness of the situation under the rug, that likely meant this entire interview was a charade.

"Nope, we're not doing this," I heard myself say.

He looked up at me, his brow furrowed.

"We have to acknowledge the weirdness to move past it."

Tyler leaned back in his chair, but didn't say a word. Fine. Don't talk dude. I will.

"Listen, what are the odds of this? Sure, it's totally reasonable that you would back into my car and we'd run into each other at the same event because we were parked there. But this?" I said, motioning back and forth between us. "This just feels unreal. But maybe it's a sign."

Tyler shook his head no, but I sensed his mood might lighten if I kept going.

"And what kind of sign do you think it is?" he asked.

"Abandon all hope, ye who enter here."

He chuckled for a second. But I didn't want him to think I wasn't interested. So I kept talking.

"Listen, we obviously didn't match in a dating sense, but I'm a great nanny, and you need someone in a hurry exactly when I'm available. So let's give this real consideration, okay?"

"Okay," he said, his face serious again. "Why is that you are available? Why did you leave your last family?"

"Great question. My former family moved to Atlanta. They asked me to join them, but Caitlyn's daughter was already eleven years old. She's very precocious. Moving all the way there, when they probably only need me another year or two, didn't seem prudent. But I miss them, and you can see Caitlyn's letter of recommendation. She told me she'd be available for a call this morning so you can do your due diligence."

He nodded, but even if he didn't show it, I knew I nailed that question. He paused and looked back down at the papers in front of him.

He looked back up at me and sighed. "Listen, you're young--"

"Thank you," I interjected. "We have that in common."

He chuckled. "That's not entirely true, but I've had nannies in the past with 15 to 30 years of experience, and they didn't last. And I think going from nanny to nanny isn't necessarily great for the kids."

"I agree. But what I will say is that a lot of times with kids who are young and energetic, let's just say, it helps to have a young nanny who can keep up with them."

He considered my answer for a moment and sighed. "My daughter is smart, but has behavioral issues. She was in foster care for a while, and I have her in therapy, but I sense that --" his voice trailed off.

"I can relate to your daughter," I confessed. "I was in foster care, and despite the hardships I endured in the system, I turned out fine. And my background has allowed me to help children like your daughter when I worked at the Casey Foster Center. I really think I'm uniquely qualified to work with your children," I said, locking eyes with him.

Tyler paused and considered my answer. "I appreciate you sharing that with me, and I agree that your experience could be very handy for our family. However, you and I already have history, and I worry we won't be able to work together."

I smiled. "Don't you think my willingness to work for you after what we've been through shows that I am a positive person who can forgive and forget? Also, despite undergoing a lot of stressors that evening, I think we both handled the situation as a team rather well."

"Well, you did just disappear and not return our telephone calls. I don't find that quality something that I'm looking for in an employee," he said.

The sharp tone of his words pissed me off, but I took a breath and calmed myself. "At the time of the incident, I didn't work for you. Plus, if you look at it from my point of view, I didn't owe you more of my time. I left because I overheard there was a news crew who wanted to speak to me, and I did not want to subject myself to that interview. Besides, I don't have to rush to return telephone calls to companies who have provided an unsatisfactory experience."

"Unsatisfactory?" He looked offended.

"Your app matched me with a date that was late who then became unfriendly after I hit the escape hatch."

"I wasn't unfriendly. I was trying to help you leave," he said.

"You helped me into the pool. But I appreciate you tried to be more friendly. Just so you know, that wasn't the experience I had of you."

"If you need someone friendly --

"I would need someone friendly for a date. I don't need a friendly boss."

"This," he said, tapping his index finger on the desk and leaning forward, "is why I don't think it'll work."

"Do you have trouble dealing with conflict? Could that be why your other nannies left you?" I asked, deliberately going on the offensive.

His eyes widened. "I have no problems dealing with conflict."

"We have conflict right here, and I suggest we resolve it and move forward. You need someone. I'm a well-qualified nanny, and denying me a job when I've done nothing wrong only compounds the wrongs I've suffered by your actions."

He threw one arm in the air and looked at the ceiling for a moment. "Wronged?"

"Do you feel you've done right? And then think whether it would it be right to deny me this position that I'm uniquely qualified for. Then factor in you need someone in a hurry and how I'm available to start right away. But you're thinking about tossing all those good reasons aside. And why? Because you backed into my car, felt awkward on our mini-date, and then we fell into a pool together--an incident you've exploited for your own gain, but one that makes my daily life only more difficult."

"You're twisting everything."

"You're denying everything. I absolutely can work with you. Can you do the same?"

He leaned forward and stared me down. His jaw set.

I worried that my temper had gotten the best of me, and that I'd gotten too aggressive. Darn.

His desk phone buzzed. "Mr. Tyler, there's a Tatiana Reynolds here to see you."

He picked up the phone right away, his face angry. "Call building security, now. She's not supposed to be within a hundred yards of here."

Tyler's door flew open, and Meredith came in. "Do you know who's in the lobby right now?"

I heard screaming in the lobby.

"I just called security," Tyler said, standing up.

"She said she saw you on the internet, and that you owe her," Meredith said.

Damn. This was bad.

"It just fucking never stops," Tyler growled.

"Get out of here," Meredith said. "Get the kids, take the nanny, catch your flight to New York."

"I can't leave now," Tyler said.

"Do you think it's a good idea that you stick around? You're better off in New York." Meredith said, retrieving a duffel bag and briefcase from next to the cabinet.

The sound of glass breaking interrupted the conversation. Oh no!

17

TYLER

The moment I heard my ex's name, my entire body pulsed with a mixture of rage, panic, and shame. My emotions threatened to overwhelm my self-control.

"Tyler, don't go out there," Meredith said, handing me my duffel and briefcase. "Don't talk to her. Don't even look at her. Exit through the back stairs."

I couldn't just leave my company to handle my own problems for me.

As if reading my mind, my sister pushed me out the door of my office toward the emergency exit stairs. "Security should've never let her up. That's why we pay them. It's not your problem."

My ex had stopped screaming, but I could hear security talking to her.

Meredith motioned for me to keep moving. "Leave early and hit the gym when you get to New York." She turned to Betty. "You're hired."

"Thanks," Betty said and then looked at me. "Don't worry. My bag is packed and in the car."

Meredith waved goodbye and shut the emergency door behind us. There was no place to go but the parking garage.

We took the stairs, and five minutes later, we exited into the garage.

Betty turned to me. "I'm on the first level. Where should I meet you?"

"I'll drive you down. You'll grab your bag, and I'll take us to the airport. The kids will meet us there."

An expression of panic spread across her face. "Will my car be okay here? It's like a million dollars every fifteen minutes."

I laughed. Finally, a simple problem. "Don't worry. I'll make sure it's fine."

"Cool."

We hopped into the car. I drove her to her car. She hopped out and snagged her bag. I popped the trunk, and she tossed it in.

Betty climbed back into the passenger seat, buckled her seat belt, and then turned t me. "Mr. Tyler--"

"Just Tyler."

"Tyler, I understand that your decision-making process was just short-circuited there. But trust me, you made the right choice. And I'd like to prove it to you. Let's commit to giving this our best effort for at the least the first ninety days. Then we'll really know if we're a good fit."

"And so you get your ninety-day bonus," I said.

"Yes, and you need to pay for my dress. Plus, you have to figure out some way to make up for the whole internet thing. Which I know wasn't your fault, but seriously. That's so embarrassing."

Her casual discussion of things made me laugh. "And what just happened in there with my screaming ex wasn't embarrassing?"

She quieted, and I glanced over at her serious face.

"What happened in there," she said, "is none of my business. I've signed a nondisclosure, and your privacy will always be safe with me. I take professional pride in that. Because now, I work for you."

"Thank you, Betty."

I drove out of the garage and stopped at a light.

Betty tapped my shoulder and held out her hand for a shake. "So, do we have a deal? Ninety days with an option?"

Could I do this? Should I do this?

"Deal," I said.

We shook on it. I guess I had a new nanny for the ninety days or until my kids ran her off.

18

BETTY

The reality of my situation hit me as we drove to the airport in silence. I was traveling to New York with a man I barely knew and kids I'd never met. But the Herzog Agency ran background checks on everyone, and I'd been in more dangerous situations than this. It's not like I had gone into a strange family before. I'd been doing it since I was six.

Tyler hit a button on his steering wheel and called someone. "Hey Mick, it's me."

"Meredith already called. Looks like you're going to New York after all, huh?"

The man's voice on the other line sounded familiar, but I couldn't place it. "I'll drive them to the airport myself," he continued. "The kids say you helped them pack their bags last night, right?"

"Yes, I did. But can you open the bags just in case to make sure they didn't take out the clothes and put their toys in them like last time?"

Mick chuckled. "Will do."

I smiled. They may be rich kids, but they were still kids.

Tyler continued to make business calls, and I allowed myself to stare out the window. I was glad to have time to just sit and think.

I glanced over at him a few times, and it amazed me how even in such a big car, he seemed almost too big to fit in the driver's seat.

The image of him with his shirt off at the hotel popped into my mind. Don't go there, Betty. I took a deep breath and zoned out until we arrived at the airport. But instead of driving to the terminal, he drove down a street I'd never seen.

Minutes later, we were exiting his SUV and stepping out onto the tarmac. We were going to New York on a private jet! Caitlyn was well-off, but she wasn't private plane rich.

Caitlyn hadn't been exaggerating. This guy did have those sweet sweet tech bucks like Zuck.

A limousine pulled up, and a familiar-looking man and two kids exited the back seat.

"Daddy!" the young boy yelled as he dragged his rolling suitcase behind him. The young girl walked over to her father as well.

As the older gentleman came closer, I realized who he was. "You're M-Forty!" I heard myself say without thinking and immediately felt stupid. He'd had a huge rap hit and married and divorced a major pop star. I always wondered what happened to him.

"You can call me Uncle M or Mick if you like," he said, holding out his hand.

I shook his hand and said, "I like the sound of Uncle M."

He chuckled and then winked at me. "I kinda do myself. I can't wait for my son, Nick, and Meredith to have kids. Then I'll be Grandpa."

"You seem too young to be a grandpa," I said.

Uncle M looked at Tyler. "Whoever she is, marry her."

Tyler's face dropped, and I laughed.

"I'm the nanny," I said.

"That's too bad," he joked. But then he leaned close to me. "They're not bad kids. They're just energetic."

I laughed. "We have that in common," I joked back.

"Not bad? Or energetic?" M-Forty asked.

"Oh, I'm bad," I joked with him, my voice low so the kids couldn't hear. "And energetic."

M-Forty laughed, and said, "that's the perfect combination."

"Enough, you two," Tyler interjected. "It's time to board the plane."

Mr. Grumpy strikes again. A member of the crew reached for my carry-on. "Can I take that for you, Miss?" he asked.

"This is my carry-on," I said.

"Yes, Miss. I'll bring it up for you."

I fought my knee-jerk reaction to feel embarrassed that I'd made some invisible faux pas.

Tyler kneeled down to talk to the kids. "Listen,

kiddos. We're going to take a trip, and I've brought your new nanny with us. So let's all say hello, okay?"

Tyler turned to me and put his hand on the little boy's back. "This little man's name is Lorenzo, but we all call him Renzo." Tyler pointed to me. "Renzo this is your new nanny, Betty."

"Hi Renzo!" I said, bending down next to him and giving him a wave.

"Hi!" he said, taking some of my hair in his hand and starting to play with it.

Tyler pulled his hand away gently and then turned to his daughter. "And this clever young lady is my daughter, Riley. Riley this is Betty."

Riley was holding a book in her hand. I stole a glance at the cover. "Roller Girl! Great choice. Astrid is having one tough summer, huh?"

Riley nodded but didn't say anything, but it was a start.

I let the kids board ahead of me so I could keep an eye on them. When I stepped into the aircraft after them, I felt way underdressed. The plane looked nicer than any place I'd ever lived with the gorgeous white sofa, wooden coffee table, and huge reclining swivel chairs. I bet one chair was worth more than my car.

My heart pounded as my face heated with feelings of being an imposter.

I'd felt this before. Like when I entered the Hollywood Roosevelt in that designer dress. Did Tyler think I was a very successful nanny? He did not know that the salary he was paying me was easily double what I had made before.

I felt stupid telling him I'd been raised in a foster home. But then again, his daughter had been in the system for a little while. It's nothing to be ashamed of. At least that's what I told myself.

But somehow, I'd always felt that being rejected by my family was branded across my face.

I pushed all those thoughts away. Why were they coming up now?

I'd done so much work on myself, and I always thought of myself as an optimistic person.

But feelings of being unworthy still ran deep.

A sense of dread regarding the hotel we'd stay at built in my stomach. My shoes, my outfit, my bargain haircut--it all seemed shabby. I couldn't imagine what it would be like in a fancy New York hotel.

I took a deep breath, fastened my seatbelt, and decided no matter how weird I felt on the inside, I wouldn't let it show on the outside. As the plane took off, I vowed not to give up. That ninety-day bonus would be mine.

19

TYLER

My ex was supposed to be in rehab again. The only way Tatiana would've gotten out would be if she'd faked her way through treatment, and then immediately started doing drugs again. What made her think that the viral video was something to get all freaked out about? Who knows? Meth logic is not something that I'd been able to figure out.

I tried not to think about how she used to be when we were in high school together. She was my first, and I thought my forever. But all that changed the summer after we graduated.

My attempts at rescuing her had failed through college and even a few times after. I'd worked hard these last five years to let her go.

I watched as the kids colored in their coloring books at their seats. My mind drifted back to the soggy coloring book that Betty had pulled out of the wet garbage bag among her things. Where had she gone that night? Did she really just run out into the night with her wet see-through dress and bare feet?

I looked over at her as she stared out the window. She was beautiful.

My heart had gone out to her when she told me she'd been in foster homes growing up. I had to make sure that I watched my rescuer tendencies with Betty. She seemed so small, fragile, and vulnerable. Not to mention her wide-eyed enthusiasm for everything. She had to be naïve.

I couldn't go around protecting her from everything. She worked for me. And I didn't have time for a relationship. I had my kids, my business, and of course my crazy ex.

Betty Abel was off-limits.

20

BETTY

It amazed me we'd flown from Los Angeles to New York so quickly.

Normally, I'd have to get to the airport hours in advance, go through security, wait to board, and all that other stuff. But today, I hopped on a plane like it was a bus.

The children were well behaved on the plane. They colored, read books, played with blocks, ate snacks, and even fell asleep.

Although, at a certain point I had to get up and stop them from turning cartwheels in the jet, because the plane was just that big.

They acted like flying on a jet was old hat.

An Escalade waited for us on the tarmac as we deplaned. I felt like a movie star. The ground crew loaded our bags into the car.

The driver held the door open for me, but I didn't get in.

"Are there car seats for the children?" I asked him.

"Yes, miss."

Out of the corner of my eye, I caught Tyler smiling. "It's not our first rodeo," he said.

"It doesn't hurt to check," I answered.

I turned back to the driver and motioned to Renzo. "Let me put the little guy into his car seat," I said, picking him up. Renzo giggled as I swung him high in the air and then balanced him on my hip.

I walked over to the car and placed the tyke into his car seat, being careful not to hit his head.

As I secured Renzo, I watched Tyler lift Riley into her booster seat on the other side of the car. Watching the care he took with his daughter melted my heart.

Once we climbed into our seats, the driver gave logistics about our ride to the hotel. My mind didn't register the boring details until I heard the driver say the words "The Plaza Hotel."

Tyler sat in the chair next to mine. "Did he say The Plaza Hotel?" I asked.

"Yes, Meredith booked it for us."

"Is your sister your assistant?" I asked.

Tyler laughed. "She is the VP of Marketing."

"Got it," I said. "So M-Forty is the kids' Grand Uncle, right?"

"Yeah, but that's a mouthful. I've known Mick my whole life though. His son, Nick, and I were best friends. He married Meredith two years ago, so we're all really close."

"Must be so nice," I said, knowing that I'd never get

married or even have true, lifelong friends. I mean, I know people, but I didn't do a great job of keeping in touch. Was it the way my brain worked? Or was it my upbringing? It was likely a mix of both.

Being a nanny was the closest I'd ever get to being part of a family, and I was fine with that.

"Have you stayed at The Plaza before?" Tyler asked.

I laughed. "I just know them from the Eloise books."

"The kids' book thing Meredith mentioned. That's why she made the reservations there. She thought the kids might like it."

"I know I will," I said, not hiding my enthusiasm.

Tyler nodded. Sometimes he was hard to read.

"Do you think they will sell a copy of the book at the hotel?" I asked. "It would be great to read it to the children."

"I'm sure. No one misses a marketing opportunity these days," Tyler said.

"You would know," I said and then realized how snarky it might sound.

Tyler chuckled. "That I would."

For a moment, we were getting along.

The kids pointed at stuff in the window and asked their dad questions. He answered every one. His patience surprised me. He hadn't acted like that with his staff.

"Are we going to have lunch soon, Dad?" Renzo asked.

"After we're settled into the hotel."

"Are you eating with us?" Riley asked.

"For lunch, but Daddy might have to work late, so you'll have to eat dinner with Betty."

"You always work late," Riley said.

I saw the flash of guilt on Tyler's face. "I'm sorry, Riley-roo. But we'll have fun at lunch."

"Do you think there will be time to visit the gift shop to buy a copy of *Eloise*?" I asked.

Tyler smiled and nodded yes. "Would you like that, kids?"

"Candy?" Renzo asked.

Tyler and I shared a look. Renzo may be young, but he understood that shopping and candy go together.

"You can have some candy, but only after dinner," Tyler said.

"Can I have one piece before?" Renzo asked.

"One piece, but not a big piece. Betty's going to make sure of that," Tyler said, looking at me.

I nodded. Tyler was testing me. A kid crying over candy wouldn't break me.

"I don't really like shopping," Riley said.

"Riley, you love shopping, and you love books," Tyler said.

She didn't reply.

"Well, do your dad a favor and go with Betty and your brother. You can pick out your own book at the store, and if they don't have one you want, I'll get you one online. Okay?"

"Okay," Riley said.

"But you both have to behave. No breaking

anything. No running indoors. If you do, no candy and no book. Is it a deal?"

Riley sighed.

"I didn't hear an answer," Tyler said. "Do we have a deal?"

"Deal!" Renzo said.

Riley waited a moment and then said, "Deal."

We rode the rest of the way in silence, but I couldn't stop smiling. I was going to stay at The Plaza!

When we pulled up to the twenty-one story historic hotel, I literally squealed with excitement without thinking. It amazed me how much it looked like I'd imagined. The flags outside, the stairs leading up to the three main doorways!

The driver opened the door, and I looked up at the historic building. "It's so beautiful!"

"Wow!" Renzo said.

I looked over to take the kids by the hand, but Tyler was already there. "Everybody stick together," he said.

We all walked up the steps together as the driver handed off our bags to one of the hotel porters.

We entered the lobby, and my mouth dropped open at the sight of the mammoth chandelier.

"Whoa, look at the light!" Riley said, pointing at the chandelier. "And the squares on the ceiling."

"Whoa!" Renzo repeated. "Square!"

I agreed with the kids. The plaster and marble coffered ceilings were major whoa.

We crossed the lobby to the front desk, and we spotted the shop.

"Dad!" Riley said, pointing to the little store. "Can we go there?"

"Let's get checked in, and that's the place where Betty's going to take you later. Okay?"

"Okay," Riley said, trying to be patient.

Tyler dealt with the check-in while the kids and I continued to marvel at the hotel.

Then I heard the woman at the front desk say, "You're booked in the Eloise and Nanny Suite."

My heart beat in my throat. The Eloise Suite!

"Sounds good. What floor is the gym on?" Tyler asked.

I laughed. He didn't care about the Eloise Suite-- just the gym. Figures.

After Tyler finished the check-in, he handed me my key, his hand brushing against mine.

A zing of excitement shivered through me. "Thanks," I said, suddenly feeling shy.

We shared a look, and then he turned to the kids.

"Renzo, take Betty's hand, and Riley, take mine. Nobody's getting lost or wandering off."

"Carry me!" Renzo said, throwing his arms up at me.

"You're a big boy. You can walk," Tyler said.

"I don't mind," I said, sweeping Renzo up into my arms. He was just on the cusp of being too big to hold. But it would be faster to carry him to the elevator than to hold his hand and risk him running off.

"If he gets heavy, which he is, put him down," Tyler said.

Renzo wrapped his arms around my neck and put his chin over my shoulder. He was so cute. Younger kids were easier to win over. I knew Riley would take a lot more to get on my side. But I had the most perfect ally in the world to win over a young girl's heart, Eloise.

21

TYLER

Watching Renzo with Betty eased my nerves. I liked Betty, but going on a business trip with both of the kids and a new nanny triggered major anxiety. And that doesn't even count my stomach churning with apprehension over Tatiana's lobby screaming.

I needed to get the kids settled and figure out a way to get to the gym to work these feelings out of my system before I exploded.

The catch was, I wondered if it was too soon to leave Betty alone with the kids. It was late afternoon East Coast time, but the kids were still on West Coast time and undoubtedly way restless. Could she handle it? Was it too big of a risk to leave her alone with the kids in New York?

We got into the elevator, and it was just the four of us. "Who wants to push the button?" Betty asked.

"I do!" Renzo said.

Oh, no! He's going to push all the buttons or take forever. I wished she hadn't asked that.

"Okay, Betty said, putting Renzo down. "We're going to the eighteenth floor. Do you know which one is eighteen?"

Renzo pointed at a random button. "That one."

"That's not quite it. I wonder if anybody else can figure it out?" Betty said aloud.

"Do you know?" she asked, turning to Riley.

Riley rolled her eyes. "Yes."

"Can you help me show your little brother? Make sure he only hits the button for the eighteenth floor. Not all the buttons."

Riley nodded and turned to her brother. "Okay, Renzo. It's the one with the one and eight. Do you know those?"

He pointed to another random button.

"Maybe you can help him press it," Betty suggested.

I admired her patience. Normally, I wouldn't do these kinds of things with the kids out in public, but we were the only people in the elevator.

Riley took Renzo's finger and pushed it on eighteen. He pushed the button a couple extra times to make sure, and Riley said, "Good job, Renzo."

Renzo clapped his hands.

"Thank you for helping me, Riley. I'm new on the job, and I might need your help training."

I could tell Riley was hiding a smile. She was a precocious kid and enjoyed being complimented for being smart.

"I think that's a good idea," I chimed in. I kneeled down and looked at Riley so we could talk eye to eye. "You've worked with a lot of nannies. Do your dad a favor and help Betty learn all our family rules."

Riley smiled, and I knew what she was thinking.

"But don't change the rules you don't like. Betty will still report to me, you know."

Riley sighed. "I know."

"What's something you think Betty should know?" I asked.

"You read books to us every night," Riley said, and then she added. "Three books." Riley looked at me to see if she'd gotten away with her three book addendum.

"As long as the books aren't too long," I added.

"Yeah, but not just one book," Riley explained. It'd been a point of contention between her and Milda.

"That's an excellent policy. One or two books just wouldn't be enough," Betty said, agreeing with Riley. "Later, we'll buy a new book downstairs. Do you have two more for tonight and some for tomorrow night?"

"We might have to repeat because Uncle M made me put my books back."

"Repeating is a suitable solution," Betty agreed.

The elevator door dinged open. Riley took her brother by the hand. "Don't run off."

She turned to Betty. "We have to hold his hand because he's little."

"I'll remember that," Betty said.

Riley paused. "You hold his other hand. Dad will hold mine."

The four of us walked down the hallway as a family.

When I opened up the door to the suite, I was treated to an onslaught of pink. It was like a flamingo exploded in here.

Riley and Renzo were psyched.

Riley dropped Betty's hand and rushed to sit on the bed. Renzo grabbed a stuffed dog off the chair and immediately started making barking noises.

"This is the nicest place I've ever been!" Riley announced, looking around the room.

"I take it this looks like the book," I said, looking at Betty.

She clasped her hands at her chest. She looked as ecstatic as the kids. "This is amazing."

"Is this is my bed?" Riley asked, bouncing up and down on the pink bed.

"Yes, you might have to share with your brother."

"Sleepover!" Betty exclaimed.

"Sleepover!" the kids repeated.

Maybe I could go to the gym after lunch. They all seemed to get along so well.

I looked at the other door and figured that's where the adjoining suites were. That's when I realized there were only two rooms. And only two beds. Damn.

22

BETTY

I remembered when I checked out *Eloise* from the school library. I'd always dreamed of having my own copy, but I never thought I'd actually be able to stay in The Plaza Hotel, let alone in Eloise's room.

From the zebra striped carpet to the chandelier, the room looked exactly like the illustrations in the book.

I marveled at the sparkly padded pink headboard with the neon lights spelling Eloise's name affixed to the wall above the bed. The kids loved it, but I deep down loved it even more.

A pink envelope on the end table caught my attention. I picked it up and turned to Tyler. "Would you mind if I opened this?"

"Sure."

I opened it. My jaw dropped open.

Tyler crossed the room and whispered in my ear, "What's wrong?"

"It's a hundred dollar gift card to the Eloise store downstairs! We can definitely buy the book and maybe some T-shirts. Do you think they have Eloise T-shirts downstairs?"

"Do you want a T-shirt, Betty?" he asked, his voice with half a laugh in it.

"I'd buy my own, of course, but it might be fun if we all got matching ones."

"Something tells me they won't have an Eloise T-shirt in my size," he joked.

My gaze drifted to his shoulders and broad chest. I turned my attention back to the envelope to stop myself from picturing him without his shirt on. There was a brochure with the gift card.

I opened it. "It says here that there's an Eloise Tea service downstairs, and story time!"

"Story time!" Riley said, rushing over. She looked up at me. "Daddy, can we go to story time?"

"I'll be busy working, but if Betty doesn't mind taking you --"

"I don't mind!" I said. "I love story time."

"I do too," Riley said, and I felt like I was this much closer to winning her over.

"You all can go in your matching T-shirts. I'll buy them for you after lunch."

"I'll buy mine, but thanks," I said, feeling silly for being so excited about getting a T-shirt.

"It's the least I can do for ruining your dress," he said.

"Don't think a T-shirt makes up for that designer

dress," I said, and gave him a playful shove. I immediately realized that was less than appropriate. What had made me do that?

Tyler gave me a light shove back. "I know. My sister told me it was some sort of vintage designer thing."

"It was a gift from my last boss."

Tyler's lips turned downward and his brow furrowed. "You let your previous family buy you a designer dress, but you won't let me buy you a T-shirt?"

He looked offended. It surprised me. "It was a going away present along with the subscription to your app. But now that I think of it, you really should buy me like two thousand shirts."

He laughed. "Well, with New York prices, it might be only a thousand."

Someone knocked on the door, and then announced, "We have your luggage."

Tyler called for the man to come in.

"Which bag to which room?" the porter asked.

Tyler motioned for me to come closer to him.

"The attached nanny suite only has one bed, so I can sleep on the couch in the living room and you can take the bed if that doesn't make you too uncomfortable."

"I can sleep on the sofa, but I'd assumed that I be sleeping in this room with the children," I said.

"You wouldn't mind?"

"I don't think it's a good idea to leave them unattended all night with a door that opens into the hall. And I don't like the idea of locking them in."

Tyler turned to one of the bellman. "Can you arrange for a rollaway bed to be brought up?"

"Yes, sir," he said.

"Then put everything but the tan bag and the duffel in this room," he said.

One porter went to Tyler's room, and the other started to unpack the kids' bags.

"I can unpack my own," I said.

Tyler shook his head. "Let them handle it, so we can all go to lunch."

"Sounds good," I said, pretending I wasn't in a panic about a strange dude unpacking my bag. Had I brought my good bras and underwear? Yikes!

As we exited the room, I made a mental note: When I got my first paycheck buy new underwear.

23

TYLER

I glanced down at my watch. I had about three hours to do lunch, shopping, and possibly a workout. Thank goodness our recruiters had booked a meeting here at the hotel.

So far, it looked like Betty could handle the kids, but I figured it was best we went out as a unit, so the kids and her would have more time getting used to each other.

It'd be too much to have them in a new environment with a new nanny without me.

The recruiter had selected about a dozen of the top graduates from NYU, Fullstack, and a few of the other coding schools. I wanted to meet with the candidates personally to vet them and to woo the best of them.

After a trip to the bathroom for the kids, and Betty shoveling a bunch of stuff into her new giant purse, we left the room. Betty pulled Renzo into her arms and carried him down the hall.

It cut down on a lot of the wandering. She put him down at the elevator and helped him press the down button. The doors dinged open. An older couple was already in the elevator.

"Riley, can you help your brother press the lobby button?" Betty asked.

Riley took her brother's hand and then looked up at Betty.

"You got it right, the one with the L for lobby," Betty encouraged.

Riley helped her brother push the button.

"Good job, Renzo!" Betty said, smiling at him, and then she turned to Riley. "Thank you, Riley."

Riley looked down at her shoes. "You're welcome."

I caught the gaze of the older woman. She smiled at me. A surge of pride swelled in my chest. Being in public with the kids hadn't always gotten me smiles from older folks.

The elevator doors opened. We exited as a family.

"There's the store!" Betty said, pointing at it as we crossed the lobby.

"It looks amazing!" Riley said.

"Amazing!" Renzo repeated.

"Let's make arrangements for lunch and then check out the shop," I suggested, knowing that I was short on time.

Betty did a great job corralling the children on the way to the restaurant. With so many new things to see, touch, and possibly destroy, Betty's idea to carry Renzo through the lobby was a good one.

When I got to the hostess station at the Palm Court, Betty whispered in my ear. "Can you ask them about the Eloise Tea?"

I knew the kids would love it, but I found it adorable that Betty seemed more excited than the kids.

"We'd like a table for four for the Eloise Tea," I said to the hostess.

"I'm sorry, sir, but we're all booked."

"Oh well," Betty said, keeping a smile on her face and turning to the children. "We'll still have fun at the store."

I would not give up so easily. "The manager, Diego, called me this morning before we left LA. He told me he'd do everything in his power to make our stay comfortable. Would you mind calling him to see if there's something you can do? Tell him it's Tyler Bronson."

"Yes, I'm sorry, Mr. Bronson. Let me make that call. Mr. Moreno and I will work this out," she said.

I read the hostess's name tag. "Thank you, Amy."

Betty looked up and shot me a pleading glance. She worried there'd be a scene. I gave her a reassuring nod, and after a couple of minutes of talking to the manager on the phone, followed by some running around, Amy returned.

"I'm sorry for the delay, Mr. Bronson. We can have a table for you in a half-hour. Will that be okay?"

"That'll be fine. We'll be in the gift shop."

Betty beamed and mouthed the words "thank you" when the hostess wasn't looking.

THE NEW SINGLE DAD BILLIONAIRE

Then she reached to pick up Renzo. I stopped her, picked up Renzo myself, and we all headed to the store.

When we got there, the store was packed with kids. I was glad I'd opted to carry Renzo.

Riley and Betty both went to the books. I followed with Renzo, giving him a toy to keep him occupied.

Betty picked up one of the books. "This one is *Eloise: A Book for Precocious Grown-ups.* Eloise is a young girl who lives here at the hotel in a room just like ours upstairs."

"What are these other ones?" Riley asked.

Betty showed her the other books in the series, and the two of them stood there with one book in their hand, trying to pick out the next one.

"We'll get them all," I said.

Riley looked at me with a shocked expression. I didn't spoil the kids with lots of stuff.

"It's a special occasion," I explained.

"What's the occasion?" Riley asked.

"It's Betty's first day of work," I said.

"Oh," Riley said, reaching over to pick up a stuffed animal. "Since it's Betty's first day at work, can I get this?"

I laughed.

Renzo grabbed a couple of toys and said, "Me!"

"Well," Betty chimed in, gazing down at a stack of pink Eloise T-shirts, "if this is a special occasion, can we have some of these?"

A store clerk approached. "Do you need any help?"

"Yes, we'll take one of each of the T-shirts." I turned to Betty. "What is your size?"

I looked back at the clerk. "We'll have one of each in medium, and then I want some for the kids, but I don't know their sizes offhand. They keep growing."

"I'll check the tags on their shirts," Betty said.

The clerk and Betty got the kids' sizes. We bought a ton of toys, and I had one of the staff bring the stuff up to our room.

Having successfully cleaned out the gift shop, we all headed back to the Palm Court for our Eloise Tea.

When we entered the Palm Court, the kids stared up at the stained glass dome ceiling. It let tons of sunlight in and that, coupled with the palm trees and high ceilings, made it seem like we were dining outside.

"Wow!" Renzo said, and then he pointed to the tribalist bar in the center of the room. "There!"

"No, bars aren't for kids," I chuckled.

"We're going to sit someplace even better," Betty said.

Betty smiled, and I could tell she was impressed by the place as well. My heart swelled. This was the most relaxed I'd felt in a long time. Betty seemed like the perfect addition to our family.

The hostess led us to our table, and Riley and Renzo spotted a tiered tray. Cupcakes, cookies and pastries packed the top-tier and tea sandwiches lined the bottom tier.

"Can we get that?" Riley asked. I knew she was referring to the sweets and not the sandwiches.

The hostess smiled. "That is on the menu for the Eloise Tea."

Oh God. The kids are going to be bouncing off the walls.

"Don't the sandwiches look fantastic!" Betty said. "They cut the crusts off and everything. So fancy!"

"Fancy!" Renzo said.

I saw what Betty was trying to do.

"Yes! The sandwiches look good," I agreed. "And so does the fruit."

"It is so sophisticated and grown-up to have sandwiches without the crust on them. Although the desserts look okay. A little babyish, but okay."

I smiled. No kid likes to be called a baby.

We ordered the Eloise Tea and all the accoutrements. Betty had sat next to me, and to my surprise, Riley sat on the other side of her. Riley had insisted on keeping one book with her instead of letting it go upstairs.

She opened it up to look at it. Normally, I wouldn't let the kids read at the table, but the food hadn't arrived.

"We're staying in her room!" Riley said, pointing to the picture.

"Isn't it exciting!" Betty agreed. "I've never been inside a book before."

"Me neither!" Riley said.

When we ordered our drinks and the sugar packed tea service, Betty leaned over and whispered in my ear.

"Do you think we could request less dessert, more sandwiches and fruit on the tray?"

Her breath on my neck distracted me, but when my mind played back what she said, I agreed.

Betty nodded and caught up with our server. She kept her eye on the children the entire time she was away from the table.

When she sat back down, Riley asked her what she was talking to the lady about.

"I asked her if she could bring us Eloise's favorite sandwiches, and she said okay."

Riley smiled and then returned to her book.

Our drinks arrived. Betty and the kids had ordered the Cold Cold Pink Lemonade.

The drinks arrived in fragile looking highball glasses. Looking at that glass sitting in front of my toddler filled me with anxiety. There was no way that glass would survive this lunch.

"Who likes Peppa Pig?" Betty asked, digging into her purse.

Renzo yelled out, "Me!"

Betty whipped out a sippy cup, commandeered his highball glass, and poured the lemonade into it.

"You're too big for a sippy cup," Betty said to Riley, "but I think you'll like this one."

Betty pulled out a plastic coffee mug that said "I like books with breakfast" on it.

Riley smiled.

With the dangerous highball glasses replaced with

THE NEW SINGLE DAD BILLIONAIRE

plastic cups, I relaxed. The tray arrived with our lunch. They'd held back on some cupcakes, but there were two giant cones of cotton candy flanking the sides of the tray.

"Daddy!" Renzo said, pointing to the cotton candy.

"If you eat your sandwiches first," I started.

Betty jumped in. "And promise to share with your father and me, plus brush your teeth when we get back to the room."

"I'll share with Dad," Riley said.

She knew I wouldn't eat much of that crap, and she wanted the most cotton candy.

Betty turned to Renzo. "Will you share with me?"

He nodded.

Lunch was one of the most fun lunches I had out with the kids since I'd had them. It had always been so difficult to keep them under control, but Betty seemed to balance the line between fun peer and authority figure so well.

After our sugar-laden lunch, Betty looked over at me. "What do you think of the idea of me taking the kids out for a little walk?"

"We'll all go," I said, deciding I'd hit the gym after my meetings.

There was a nice shopping plaza on the same block as the hotel. We window shopped and talked. The kids skipped and buzzed around on their sugar high.

The conversation between Betty and the kids flowed easily. Betty knew all the kids' shows and understood all the references. I made a mental note to learn more about the kids' interests.

My cell phone buzzed. I hated checking it, but it could be urgent. It was a text from Reece. She said the recruiter and candidates were waiting for me. Holy shit! I lost track of time.

24

BETTY

*S*o far, my first day was going well, and I wanted to keep it that way.

The kids relished their father's attention, and Tyler seemed to enjoy our window-shop walking session as well. The kids had tried to get him to buy them more stuff, but he quelled that quickly.

I appreciated he understood how to discipline his kids. It made my job easier.

We stopped for a moment so Tyler could check his telephone.

"I've got to go potty!" Renzo said.

I looked around the shopping plaza for a restroom sign, but I didn't see one.

"Shit!" Tyler said.

"Shit!" Renzo repeated.

"Daddy didn't mean to say that. We don't say that," Tyler corrected, but his mind was somewhere else.

"We're not supposed to swear," Riley added.

"What's wrong?" I asked Tyler.

"I'm late for my meeting."

"I'll take Renzo and Riley to the bathroom and then back to the room." I said.

"I'm sorry, Betty. But I'm just not comfortable with you and the children being out in New York."

I understood. "Let's all hurry back to the hotel, and Renzo, you can use the potty in the room."

We took the kids by the hands and walked back briskly.

"I really have to go," Renzo said.

"He refused to wear his pull-ups, so we better make it quick," Tyler said.

I had an idea. I bent down to talk to Renzo. "Want a piggyback ride?"

"Yeah!" he said, jumping onto my back.

"Now we can go really fast," I said, trotting toward the shopping plaza exit. "We'll beat Daddy and Riley."

I glanced back at Tyler. "No, you won't!" he said, taking the bait.

In two seconds, Riley was on his back, and we raced onto the street.

"Faster, Daddy!" Riley yelled, laughing.

Tyler caught up with me. "Do you think you can make it all the way there?" He asked.

I faked like I was breathing heavily and slowed down. Tyler slowed down and had a concerned look on his face.

"Psych!" I yelled and then tore down the street.

I heard Tyler's heavy footsteps behind me. A crowd

of people tried to get in our way, but I saw a small opening, and I pushed through.

I knew that would be harder for Tyler. This was my chance to win.

"You'll never catch us!" I yelled back.

"Don't be so sure!" Tyler said as he passed me.

Damn.

The kids roared with laughter.

Tyler could have easily beat me, but he slowed his run to keep it close.

"They're catching up, Daddy! Hurry!" Riley shrieked.

Renzo laughed some more, and then he said, "Sorry!"

Running toward the hotel, I didn't register what he meant until I felt a wetness down my back.

Oh no! All the bouncing and laughing made Renzo pee. I should've known better!

25

TYLER

I needed to get to my meeting, but I hated to leave. It wasn't like me to be late, and it wasn't like me to want to ditch work, and a workout before.

"Wave goodbye to Daddy," Betty said, as I stepped off the elevator on the eleventh floor. Renzo was still on Betty's back.

The excitement must've tuckered him out because he was quiet.

"Bye kids!" I said. "Listen to Betty while I'm gone. Be good."

"Bye, Daddy!" Riley said as the elevator doors closed.

I headed to the Executive Boardroom, but I didn't rush. They could wait, and I needed to get my head in the game. I'd told Alan, our recruiter, to start the presentation we'd prepared for the candidates.

When I entered the boardroom, he'd done as I asked, and the presentation was just wrapping up. It looked as if I'd arrived as planned.

Alan finished up the last couple of minutes of the presentation and then introduced me. I shook hands with each of the candidates and allowed Alan to lead the discussion.

I wanted to see how our main East Coast recruiter handled himself in these sessions. The caliber of new hires hadn't met my standard.

My mind kept going back to Betty and the kids. She impressed me with that piggyback race. She had a point about being young and having the energy to keep up with the kids.

Milda could've never pulled that off.

"Boss man likes that answer," Alan said, interrupting my thoughts.

I must've been smiling, thinking about the kids. "You might say that," I said noncommittally. I hated being called "boss man."

I forced myself to pay attention to the meeting.

The plan was, if I liked any of the candidates, I was to signal Alan by saying let's discuss this over dinner. Except I wanted to be with Betty and the kids for dinner.

I caught myself hoping that none of these applicants were acceptable, but fate foiled my plan.

"Let's discuss this further over dinner downstairs," I suggested.

Alan stood up, and the candidates seemed excited.

They all were pretty decent, but there were four for sure that I wanted. The other eight could try to impress me at dinner. Maybe they have a chance.

I wished I was going home to have dinner with Betty and the kids. Thinking of the hotel as "home" struck me as odd. I'd bought an enormous house when the company went public, but the only thing about it that was homey was the kids.

What made the hotel room that we'd spent less than five minutes in feel like home?

My brain knew the answer: Betty.

As we exited the boardroom, I pulled Alan aside to let him know that Jeff, Sasha, Jorge and Suresh were the top candidates.

"I'll make sure they're seated closest to you," he said.

"Very good," I said, pulling out my phone. "I just need to place a call to check up on my kids. I'll catch up with you all in a moment."

Alan led the recruits downstairs, and I stepped away to make my call.

I noticed there was a text message from a number I didn't recognize. It was Betty! I hadn't put her number in my phone yet.

The message read: *It's Betty. I called the office and got your cell phone number so you'd have mine. Everything is great. We are in the room. Do you want me to order you anything from room service?*

I texted back. *No, but thanks for asking. I'm having*

dinner out. I'll try to get back before you put the kids to bed, but if I'm not, make sure they're in bed by eight.

She texted back, "will do," almost instantly.

I put my phone back into my jacket pocket as I headed to the elevators. If I hurried this along, I might finish in time to put the kids to bed with Betty.

26

BETTY

I'd bathed and changed Renzo into his pajamas the moment we'd returned to our room. I hadn't dared to leave the kids alone to take a shower. So I'd made do by toweling off and changing into an old T-shirt.

I put the kids to bed in the Eloise Suite after reading four stories, which went a long way to winning Riley over to my side.

Then, I went into the living room of the adjoining nanny suite to put the sofa cushions we'd commandeered for pillow forts back before Tyler returned.

My first evening alone with the kids seemed successful. It disappointed them when Tyler called to say he was working late.

We'd had a good night. The kids were well behaved, mostly. I tuckered them out with leapfrog and playing airplane. When it came time to eat their vegetables, I bribed them that they could eat dinner in our pillow forts if they finished them all.

It'd been a hit.

Damn, I needed a shower. I wreaked from the running, playing, and the toddler pee. The catch was that if I showered in the Eloise Suite, I'd wake up the children.

But if I showered in Tyler's ensuite bathroom, I might not hear the kids if they woke up.

I waited a half hour to make sure they were sound asleep. Since my stuff was unpacked in their room, I grabbed an Eloise T-shirt and rushed to Tyler's bathroom for a quick shower.

When I entered, it amazed me at how nice it was. The floral mosaic tiles gave the room such a lux feel, and the clawfoot tub called to me. But I needed to hurry, so I stripped off my clothes, jumped in the shower, and rushed to clean off.

I had rinsed off my hair and my back when I heard a noise coming from the other room. Was that the door opening? Had one kid woken up and left the room?

I hopped out of the shower, threw the house robe around me without even toweling off, and dashed out of the bathroom, trying to find the tie to the robe so I could fasten it as I ran.

My hand found one end of the robe closure, but not the other. I looked down to find it and my head smacked straight into what I later realized was Tyler's chest.

I stepped back, stunned. My brain registered that my robe was wide open just as he yelled.

"Fuck!" Tyler said, turning around and hiding his eyes. "I didn't know you were in here. I thought you were asleep in the kids' room."

Holy smokes! I just flashed my new boss.

27

TYLER

Even though the children should've been in bed by now, I still hoped they were up. They were still on California time, and they'd had a week's worth of sugar in one afternoon.

Riding in the elevator, I couldn't help but look at the buttons and remember Betty with the kids earlier today. It was such a simple thing, but those types of things went a long way with kids.

The arrangement with Betty just might work.

Although, the ultimate test would be how she handled them while I was gone. The children were always more well behaved when I was around, but from what I can tell from the other nannies, they went from Jekyll to Hyde the moment I left.

I stepped off the elevator, relieved that Betty wasn't locked in the hall. The lack of emergency phone calls or fire alarms meant Betty had fared better than most nannies so far.

I entered my suite. It was empty. I opened the adjoining door and peeked into the kids' room. The lights were out. Everyone was in bed.

I closed the door. A pang of disappointment stabbed at my chest. I thought, at the very least, Betty would still be awake.

Well, at least I could get to the gym tonight. I headed into my bedroom to get my gym bag. I heard a scuffling noise in the bathroom, and half a breath later, Betty dashed out of the bathroom and ran straight into me.

She stepped back, and it took me a moment to register that her robe was all the way open.

I caught an eyeful of her wet, naked body and then turned away uttering something random.

She was saying something, but I was too distracted to hear what she was saying. My mind couldn't stop thinking about how good she looked. My dick hardened at the idea that she was naked in my room right now.

What the fuck? I wasn't some teenager. She was embarrassed enough, and I didn't need to make the situation even more awkward by turning around and sporting a giant woody.

"I'll let you get dressed," I said, heading for the living room to calm myself.

I closed the door behind me, paced for a moment, but that didn't get my dick under control. Sitting was my best option. I adjusted myself in my pants and took care as I sat down on the sofa.

Come on, man. Pull yourself together. I know it's been a while, but damn. Don't be a creep here. She works for you.

I thought about work shit to take my mind off the sight of Betty naked. She looked so good. Great tits, nice rounded thighs. An actual bush instead of being waxed to the hilt like everyone did these days. Naturally beautiful.

Fuck.

I decided that I'd wait here for her, but only talk for a minute to stave off the awkwardness, and then hit the gym to work off this energy. I heard the door open. She stood in the doorway, wearing one of the Eloise T-shirts I'd bought her, and a pair of shorts. No bra.

Okay, we'd talk for more than two minutes. There was no way I was going to stand up right now.

28

BETTY

I rushed back into the bathroom. All I wanted to do was crawl into a hole, but there wasn't one available. I decided I would get dressed, feign exhaustion, and hide in the kids' room until morning.

I slipped on my fresh Eloise T-shirt and shorts then headed to the living room. When I opened the door to the living room, I spotted Tyler on the elegant gray sofa, staring out the large windows overlooking the New York skyline.

His pinched, almost pained expression let me know he was not happy. He couldn't be thinking of firing me, could he?

Not for the accident in there, but maybe for leaving the children unattended. Why hadn't I waited until he came home to shower?

I lingered in the doorway that divided the bedroom from the living room. Tyler looked over at me.

"Sorry I flashed you," I joked, trying to break the tension.

His face remained serious. "I don't know what you're talking about."

Wait, what? Was that a joke? It had to be, right? But now, I'd missed the opportunity to laugh.

A beat of awkward silence compelled me to babble an explanation. "You said you'd be late, and I needed to take a quick shower. I used yours to not wake up the kids. But when I heard the noise, I thought it might be Renzo or Riley."

"No need to explain, and don't worry, I didn't see," he paused, looked down, and appeared to be fighting a smile, "much."

His embarrassment, coupled with relief that I wasn't getting fired, and the craziness of the moment exploded out of me as laughter. "You saw everything!"

He laughed. "Well, not everything," he said, emphasizing every.

I shook my head and put my hand on my face. "And I thought Renzo peeing on me was going to be the most awkward thing that happened to me today."

"Wait, what?" Tyler asked, still chuckling.

"He didn't make it to the room during our piggyback race. Bouncing him around so much wasn't the best plan, as it turns out."

"That was five hours ago, and you're just showering now?"

"I couldn't risk leaving them alone, and luckily, I

had a multitude of fresh T-shirts waiting for me," I said, tugging at the top of my new Eloise shirt.

Tyler's eyes drifted to my chest and lingered for a moment. My nipples hardened, but it had to be from the cold.

A knock on the door interrupted us.

"Room service," a male voice called out from the hall.

I shot Tyler a questioning look. "Did you order something to eat?"

He shook his head no as he strode to the door to check it. I followed behind him.

Tyler opened the door to find a porter with champagne and chocolate-covered strawberries.

"I think you've got the wrong room," Tyler said.

"No, it's the Eloise Suite. I took the lady's call myself fifteen minutes ago," the porter said, looking at me.

Tyler and the porter turned to me.

My hands shot to my mouth. "Oh, no!"

Tyler raised an eyebrow.

"Eloise ordered champagne in the book I read them tonight!"

Just when I thought I'd saved my first day on the job, I stumbled again.

29

TYLER

*E*verything about this incident screamed Riley. It impressed me she'd figured out how an old school hotel phone worked from an illustrated book. She learned things fast.

"Riley!" I called out, heading to the room.

Betty shushed me. I turned to look at her.

"You'll wake up, Renzo," she whispered.

She was right. Waking him up and having him see chocolate would make it impossible to get him back to sleep.

I took a deep breath, opened the door slowly, and entered the room, keeping my footsteps light.

I could tell by the quick sound of the covers shuffling and how she was turned facing away from the door, she was pretending to sleep.

I went to her side of the bed. "Don't pretend you're sleeping," I whisper-shouted.

"What's that, Daddy?" she asked, blinking and putting on her cutest innocent face.

But that adorable face wouldn't work on me. I pulled down the covers and carried her into the living room, so I wouldn't make any noise.

The porter had brought the cart inside.

Seeing the cart, Riley squealed with delight. "It worked!"

I put her down and kneeled in front of her. "Riley, you should know you're not allowed to order things to the room or eat late at night."

She looked at the floor. "Maybe we can just drink the campaign and save the rest for breakfast."

I fought a smile at her mixing up the word for champagne. "Champagne," I said, emphasizing the correct pronunciation, "is not for real life children. No alcohol until you're thirty, understand?"

She nodded yes.

"Okay, now apologize to the man for wasting his time," I said, turning her little body toward the porter.

Riley took a deep breath and looked up at the man. I'd taught her that apologies needed to have two main parts: looking the person in the eye so they know you mean it, and the words 'I'm sorry' and 'I was wrong.'"

"I'm sorry for wasting your time. I was wrong. It won't happen again."

She'd added the 'it won't happen again' on her own, and it impressed me.

The porter smiled. "Thank you. You are more than forgiven."

She looked over at me, hopeful that her apology had met my approval.

"Okay, Riley-roo. Time for bed and don't wake up your brother."

Riley went to bed, and I returned my attention to the porter.

"Shall I take this away, sir?"

I'd planned to go to the gym, but I didn't feel like it. The strawberries looked good. A little dessert and a getting-to-know each other chat was probably in order for Betty and me.

I turned to Betty. "Do you like strawberries?"

She smiled. "I'd hate for them to go to waste."

I turned back to the porter. "Leave it here."

30

BETTY

The porter set the champagne and fruit on the living room coffee table and left.

I needed to relax and make a good impression. I just wasn't certain how I'd pull it off.

"Shall we sit down?" I asked, feeling awkward. Why the hell had I used the word shall?

"Would you mind if I changed into something more comfortable?" Tyler said. He must've realized what it sounded like, because he motioned to my outfit and added, "I just meant shorts and a T-shirt."

"Well, you didn't pick up one as snazzy as this downstairs, but whatever you've got will have to do," I said, hoping to sound breezy and fun, but not feeling like that at all.

Tyler chuckled and left the room.

I sat on the couch and tried to look calm. I'd never drank champagne before. Most of the time I drank whatever the kids were having, which was mostly water and apple juice.

But I was definitely going to drink that champagne. God knows how much it cost, and I didn't want the refreshments to go to waste. Riley ordering it was my fault. I'd put the idea in her head, and I'd left her alone in the room with the phone.

I smiled. Riley was confident and smart. I'd never have had the guts to order room service at her age.

I heard the bedroom door open, and I looked over to say hello. He'd changed into baggy shorts and a muscle tee with the brand name "Barbell" emblazoned on the front. He looked like he was ready to go to the gym.

I marveled at all the veins in his shoulders and arms. Pretty much everywhere.

"My eyes are up here," Tyler said.

Yikes! I must've been staring. My eyes shot to his. "I'm so sorry."

Tyler laughed. "I get it all the time. Mostly from dudes, but women, too."

"You must work out a lot," I said.

"Nah," he said sarcastically.

I chuckled at his joke, appreciating the lightened mood.

He sat on the couch with me, but on the other side to keep a respectful distance. Although, with his size, he took up half of the middle cushion, too.

He motioned to the strawberries. "Should we go for it?"

"Yes, after you."

"Ladies first."

I sized up all the strawberries and picked the biggest one.

"Good choice," he said, taking the little one.

"Wimp."

"I'm watching my figure," he said.

I chomped on my strawberry and realized that I should've taken a plate. Then, I didn't know what to do with the little green top. Why was I so awkward?

Tyler stood up and reached for the champagne. "I don't do this often, but let me give it a go."

He removed the gold metal foil and then struggled with the cork. "Maybe I should've let the porter handle this," he said. I turned away so that I wouldn't stare at his biceps.

He definitely looked good in a tank top. I didn't realize just how muscular he was in his suit.

The popping sound of the cork made me jump, but the champagne didn't fizzle over and make a mess like it does in the movies.

"Good job," I said, clapping. Then I realized how ridiculous I was. "Sorry, it's a habit. Kids need lots of encouragement."

"It feels good. Maybe dads need lots of encouragement, too. Come to think of it, maybe nannies do as well."

Tyler poured the champagne, handed me a glass, and sat back down on the couch. This time a little closer to me. He turned to me and held up a glass. "Let's toast to a successful first day on the job."

I smiled as we clinked glasses. He considered today a success!

I sipped the champagne and forced myself not to wince. It was so dry and un-sweet. My brain correlated carbonation with soda. I had the fashion sense and palate of an eight-year-old.

I grabbed another strawberry, gobbled it, and then sipped more champagne. The sweetness of the chocolate-covered strawberries made the champagne taste better.

"So, how was your meeting?" I asked, wanting to break the silence.

"It was good. We might actually get a couple of decent coders out of it. How was your time with the kids?"

"Great! We read four books, made pillow forts, leapfrogged, played airplane, and ate dinner. And don't worry, Riley told me they had to eat their vegetables, and that corn didn't count."

"She actually told you that?"

"She takes training me seriously," I said, taking another gulp of champagne. It was starting to taste good.

"I'm glad. Let's just say Riley and other nannies don't exactly get along."

"I was like her as a kid. I hated how people talked down to me. She's smart and has her own thoughts.

You've got to give respect in order to get respect, even with kids."

Tyler's expression softened, and he looked me right in the eye. "That's true. You really do."

Wow! With his square jaw, thick light brown hair, and amazing body, Tyler was obviously a hottie. But in this second, he was more than that.

His sincerity disarmed me. The temperamental grump that I'd seen barking orders at the Roosevelt had been replaced with someone kind and soulful.

I looked away, worried that I'd been staring again. The elegance of the room and the champagne made sitting here feel intimate and date-like.

Not knowing what to do, I grabbed another strawberry and gulped some more champagne. "These are good."

"I'm glad you like them," he said, his voice deep and rumbly.

My face heated, and I became acutely aware of the distance between his bare, muscled arms and mine.

Neither of us talked for a moment. My heartbeat sped up.

Tyler cleared his throat and reached for the champagne bottle and motioned to my empty glass. "Did you want more?"

I wasn't thirsty, but it was something to do, and I didn't want the champagne to go to waste. "Thanks."

He filled my glass, and I took another big swig. It tasted better than the last glass, and it relaxed me.

"So, what made you want to be a nanny?" Tyler asked.

"I'd always dreamed about being placed with a well-off family when I was in the system, but that never happened. I started babysitting when I was sixteen for a nice family. It felt so good that I thought, this is what I want to do. It's been great."

"That's why you love all the kids' stuff, hmmm? You get to enjoy the stuff you never had growing up."

My eyes welled with tears, and I felt stupid for revealing so much. Why had I done that? "I'm just a kid at heart," I answered, trying to lighten the mood.

I turned to look out the window. I didn't want Tyler to see my watery eyes. Pull it together, Betty.

"Is there a balcony out there?" I asked.

Tyler stood up. "Yes, why don't we check it out?"

A change of venue sounded perfect.

I stood up, but I felt super dizzy. My toe hit something on the floor as I tried to find my footing. I lost my balance, and it looked like I was going to face-plant right on the coffee table.

31

TYLER

Betty swayed as she stood up. She took a step to steady herself and tripped on my foot. I grabbed her before she fell onto the coffee table.

"Whoops!" I said. "Are you okay?"

I had my arms around her to keep her from falling, her shoulder leaned against my chest. She turned toward me and looked up. Her long eyelashes blinking.

"Nice catch," she said, her voice a sexy whisper. The feeling of one of her tits pushed against me along with that voice and that look made my cock stir.

This girl was effortlessly sexy.

She put her hands on my arms to regain her footing and giggled. "So big. And hard," she said, running her hands on my biceps.

She was drunk, but damn. This girl was killing me.

"Let's check out that view," she said, tottering over to the sliding glass doors.

I stayed close to make sure she didn't stumble again.

THE NEW SINGLE DAD BILLIONAIRE

We stepped out onto the balcony, and I slid the glass door shut behind us. She swayed on her feet, and I put my hand on her back to steady her. "Easy, easy."

She'd only had two glasses of champagne, and she was already tipsy. Cute, but dangerous.

She giggled. "We're up so high!"

"Have you been to New York before?"

"I've barely been anywhere," she said. "This is amazing."

I looked down at her as she stared at the New York skyline. She let her head rest against me. A warm summer breeze blew across my face. A giddy feeling shivered through my body. I'd only had one glass of champagne, and I weighed over two hundred pounds. I couldn't be drunk, could I? Maybe it was the drink and the sugar from the dessert. I rarely ate sweets.

But I doubted that was the reason. This fluttery feeling in my chest was because of Betty.

I leaned down to kiss the top of her head and stopped myself. This wasn't a date. This was my nanny.

I couldn't be the creep who took advantage of a young, drunk girl who worked for him.

"It's time for me to get to bed. Are you going to be all right getting to your room? You seem a little wobbly on your feet."

Her mouth dropped open. I could tell the sudden ending of the evening took her by surprise.

"I think the champagne just went to my head. I'll clean up and get to bed," she said.

"The staff will take care of it. I think it's best we both get some sleep."

She nodded, and not wanting her to see that I'd gotten hard just standing there with her, I turned around and went straight to my room. From now on, no more drinking with the nanny. I had to keep it professional.

32

BETTY

I laid in bed feeling like a total idiot. I'd avoided getting in trouble for most of yesterday's disasters, and then I blew it by getting drunk.

So big! So hard! I'd said that out loud to my boss while feeling up his biceps. No wonder he left so suddenly.

Today I'd be the calm, cool professional nanny that I knew I could be. I promised the kids that we would go downstairs for story time if their dad said it was okay.

I'd make sure that Tyler didn't have to worry about a thing.

I rolled over, just as the kids were waking up.

My head ached. Was this a hangover? I'd only been drunk twice in my life, and I'd never gotten a hangover.

Maybe it was the combination of the flight yesterday and the champagne. I'd only been on a plane twice as well.

I took a deep breath and plotted out what I needed to do: get the kids ready, get them some breakfast, and get some coffee for me.

A gentle knock sounded on the door.

Renzo jumped out of bed and ran over to open it. "Daddy!"

"It's okay if I come in?" Tyler asked, looking at me.

Did he think I was in bed naked in the same room as the kids or something? How bad of an impression had I made last night?

"Of course," I said, getting out of bed so he could see that I was wearing the same shorts and T-shirt from last night. Nothing inappropriate.

"I called downstairs to get some coffee for myself, and I got extra for you if you want it," he said.

"Thank you," I said.

"You were up late after a long day, so I thought I'd bring the kids downstairs for breakfast, and give you time to relax and get ready for the trip home."

"We can't go home! We're going to story time!" Riley yelled.

"I said we would go if it was okay with your father," I said, realizing I'd screwed up by not running it by Tyler first.

Tyler looked over at me. "What time does it start?"

"They do it at 10:30, noon, and 2 o'clock."

"I'll take the kids to the 10:30 one. Do you want to meet us down there?"

"Absolutely."

"Can I wear my new Eloise dress?" Riley asked.

"I think this is the perfect occasion for it," Tyler said. "Betty, can you help Riley get into her new dress? And I'll help this one," he added, bending down to tickle Renzo.

"Sounds good," I said, making the bed.

"The hotel staff will take care of that. Just give me a hand so I can get them to breakfast in plenty of time."

"Of course," I said, feeling sheepish. I wasn't used to people picking up after me. But it was important that I get these kids dressed and ready to go.

Tyler and I ended up in front of the dresser drawer at the same time. I smelled his aftershave, and his arm brushed against mine.

The stupid thing I said about his biceps flooded back to me. I couldn't find Riley's new dress, and I worried Tyler would see me blush.

Then I realized the porter probably hung it in the closet.

It was as if I couldn't think straight around Tyler.

I grabbed the pink tutu dress out of the closet and helped Riley get dressed. She looked adorable.

She rushed to look at herself in the mirror. "I look just like Eloise."

"Except prettier," Tyler added.

Riley smiled.

We finished dressing the kids, and Tyler looked over at me. "Now you have some time to yourself to shower and change. Order breakfast from room service. There is aspirin in the medicine cabinet of my suite, if you need it."

He winked at me. He knew I had a hangover.

"Thanks. I'll see you guys at story time."

The three of them left, and I let out a sigh of relief. At least I hadn't lost my job, but I felt so embarrassed.

I showered, got ready, and let in the hotel staff to clean the room.

Once the housekeeping staff left, I took some selfies of me in the room. This might be my only chance to stay in a hotel this nice, and I wanted to remember it forever.

Thanks to the coffee, aspirin, and shower, my hangover had faded, and the excitement of story time at The Plaza had overtaken my embarrassment.

Tyler had winked at me regarding my hangover, so obviously it couldn't be that big of a deal. Right?

I entered the lobby just as the kids and Tyler exited the Palm Court restaurant.

"Betty!" Riley called out to me. "It's story time!"

"It is!" I said, grateful that I was winning her over.

The four of us entered the gift shop.

I was glad we were fifteen minutes early, so we could get a good seat even if it was just spaces on the floor.

"Where should we go for story time?" I asked one employee.

"We only do story time on Saturdays," he said.

"But the brochure said that there were three times today."

"I'm sorry, you must've gotten an old one," he said.

I looked over at Renzo and Riley. Renzo didn't seem

to be bothered, but Riley frowned at me and folded her arms. She was too young to understand that it wasn't my fault. I knew what it was like to have adults not keep their promises.

"Is there some way we can do a shorter story time for the kids?" I pressed.

"We have some of the activity books that you can take home," he said.

I looked around the store, and I saw the little stage. "Couldn't someone just hop up there and read one quick story?"

"I'm the only person working right now."

"You can read it!" Riley said, tugging at my shirt. Then she looked over at the store clerk. "She's a good reader. She does voices and everything."

"You're welcome to use the stage," the clerk said.

A woman with four kids came in. "Is there story time today?"

The clerk looked at me. Oh, my gosh! It was one thing to read to two kids in private, but it was a whole other thing to read in public.

I looked over at Riley, and her eyebrows were raised high, and her mouth hung open. There was no way I could say no.

"Yes, there is a story time today," I said, digging into my bag and pulling out a tiara I usually used to play princesses. After all, you can't be in charge of story time wearing just regular clothes. You've got to dress for the part.

The store clerk handed me a copy of *Eloise*, along

with the activity books he mentioned. "There's a room over there with a table for the activity after."

Okay, then. Time to get started. Even though I was shaking on the inside, I vowed to nail this story time and make Riley proud.

33

TYLER

When I'd originally heard about story time, I wasn't too happy. I needed to get home and find out what happened with Tatiana and get back to the office.

But the kids seemed so excited, and I wanted them to get along with Betty, so I acquiesced. I thought for sure there'd be tears when they found out there was no story time.

Betty stepping up to the plate and making it happen impressed me. I could tell it went a long way impressing Riley as well.

Betty looked adorable with her tiara on, and I took a seat next to the kids.

A crowd of people gathered, and I could tell that Betty was nervous. I gave her an encouraging smile. She sat up straight, pulled her shoulders back, and took a deep breath.

"Gather around everyone. We are about to begin. As

you probably know, you're in the hotel that Eloise herself lives in with her nanny.

"And Betty's my nanny!" Riley called out.

My heart soared.

The other kids nodded, and Betty smiled. "That's right. I'm your nanny and your brother's too."

Betty began reading the story, and the children were riveted. My phone buzzed against my chest. I reached into my pocket. It was Alan, the recruiter.

I knew it might be urgent, but I didn't want to miss what was happening in front of me. Even though it was just our new nanny reading a story, somehow it felt important.

I declined the call and sent him a text. *Call you in an hour.*

Story time was about family, and I wasn't going to miss it.

34

BETTY

I sat in my room and debated what to do. It was my day off, and the house was empty. M-Forty had taken the kids to a birthday party, and Tyler had gone to work.

I wanted to take a dip in the hot tub, but, even though Tyler said I could use the pool or spa anytime I wanted, I didn't feel comfortable making myself at home here.

It'd been two months with the family, but I still wasn't used to living in such an expensive house.

The property was what they called the Balinese-style Malibu Villa, and it overlooked the Santa Monica Bay. The place had an enormous deck with a cabana, spa, and a gorgeous garden with a waterfall.

It was like living in a magazine.

I'd been saving as much money as I could, just in case the end of our ninety-day agreement meant the end of the line for me.

Renzo and I got along like best buds, and Riley continued to warm to me. Tyler and I seemed to get along, but we rarely interacted without the kids.

He worked long hours, but he came home every night to put the kids to bed when he could. After the kids were asleep, he'd disappear to his side of the house.

The only time he came to my side of the house was to use the home gym next to my room. He worried that the noise of him working out would bother me, but it didn't at all. Well, it did bother me, but more in the "hot and bothered" way, not the annoyed way.

I'd never been into the muscle-bound type, but there was something about how tough he looked on the outside and then how tender he was with his kids that really got to me.

But having a crush on my boss was the worst thing I could do. I needed to get over that. I'd avoided any more embarrassing incidents since that first night, and I wanted to keep that going.

Although, now that I thought of it, Tyler and I hadn't been alone together at all since that night. The kids were always around, and he always went to his wing of the house when they went to bed. Was he avoiding me?

Nope. Not going to think about it. It was my day off, and I needed to relax. My shoulders were aching from carrying Renzo way too much. It'd only been a month, but I swear he'd grown.

Since it was fall, Riley had returned to school. She'd

THE NEW SINGLE DAD BILLIONAIRE

been having trouble here and there, but nothing too out of control. Both the kids went to therapy, but Tyler always took them and I knew little about it. I figured he would tell me if I needed to know.

It was the middle of October, and it was a little chilly out. But it was perfect hot tub weather, and it being Malibu, the sun was bright. Yeah, it was time to make myself at home and go for it.

I rifled through my drawer and looked for my one-piece swimsuit. It was my go-to swimsuit when I was too embarrassed to wear my bikini, which was most days. I pulled out my one piece, but the seat of the suit was so worn that it was see-through, and it sported a hole in a very inopportune spot.

I tossed it in the trash. That only left my bikini, but I hadn't exactly shaved enough to wear the bikini.

Tyler and the kids wouldn't be home for hours, and I could bring a big beach towel with me just in case. So, I slipped into my bikini and flip-flops and headed for the deck.

There was a strong breeze off the ocean that made the day a little chilly. Fall was coming, and it was my favorite season. Despite the chill, I knew I'd be warm in the hot tub.

I hit the button to start up the jets and to open the automatic cover, put my towel next to the stairs, and lowered myself in.

Wow! I should've done this so much sooner. The warm water felt amazing, and the jets in this hot tub felt like thousands of warm fingers massaging every inch of my body.

I looked out at the Pacific Ocean. This was really living! A gust of wind blew my towel a few feet away, but luckily it caught on the leg of a piece of deck furniture. It wasn't far.

I maneuvered my body so that my sore shoulder was right in front of the jets, relaxed, and closed my eyes. A scuffling sound not far from me put me on high alert.

My eyes popped open, and I sat up. I hadn't heard him come out onto the deck. He must have used the sliding glass doors just off of his room.

"I'm sorry," I said. "I didn't think you'd be home, and you said I could use the hot tub."

"It's not a problem. I can come back later."

"Stay!" I said, feeling terrible for chasing the man out of his own hot tub. "I'll go."

I went to get out of the water, and then I remembered my bikini bottoms. The towel was just out of reach. Damn it!

35

TYLER

I'd gone into the office to meet with the private investigator to find out what was going on with Tatiana. After the incident last month, she'd disappeared.

I didn't care what happened to her. What I needed to know was whether she had something up her sleeve regarding the custody of the kids--particularly Riley.

The court had awarded custody of Renzo to me easily, but when I learned he had a half sister, it took a while to find Tatiana. The entire duration of our off and on relationship, Tatiana never mentioned having a daughter. Judging from Riley's age, Tatiana must've had her during one of her many ghosting incidents.

Riley's adoption was in progress, and even though the court had severed Tatiana's parental rights, I worried she'd figure out a way to sabotage our life.

The investigator told me she'd been living in some cheap hotel in Baja with some dude, who was a suspected drug dealer. But as far as her scheming to get the kids back, there wasn't any information.

As I pulled up to the house, I decided that a dip in the hot tub would ease the ache in my back from all the stress. I pulled into the garage, walked across the lawn, and entered through the kitchen door.

The house was quiet. A twinge of loneliness struck me. No kids. No Betty. Big empty house. I sighed, grabbed a bottled water from the kitchen, and headed to my room to change into my trunks and T-shirt since it was chilly outside.

Two minutes later, I stepped out onto the deck and spotted Betty in the hot tub. Her eyes were closed with her mouth open slightly as she relaxed in the water. My eyes took in the sight of her in that tiny bikini.

Fuck!

I must've made some kind of noise, because her eyes shot open, and she looked straight at me.

Betty volunteered to leave, but I wouldn't dream of having her leave just because I couldn't handle seeing her in a swimsuit. A very tiny swimsuit.

"No, don't. I wouldn't enjoy it anyway, knowing I kicked you out," I said.

"There's plenty of room. Why can't we share?"

"If you're sure you don't mind."

"Of course not."

"Cool," I said, trying to act calm even though my breathing had gone a tad ragged.

I turned my back to her and forced my dick to calm down as I took my shirt off.

When I turned around to face her, she looked away. I smiled. Okay, so it wasn't so easy for her either. But if she could handle it, I could.

I walked over to the edge of the spa and eased myself into the warm water. "Ah. That feels so good. My back is a little sore from all the time at the desk."

"Yeah, it feels great. My shoulders are a little sore from carrying around Renzo," she said. "He's getting big."

I nodded and tried not to look at her tits in that little bikini. The way the spa jets were making them jiggle made it rough.

We sat in the hot water, avoiding looking at each other for a few minutes.

This was so fucking awkward. How long should I sit before it didn't seem insulting to leave?

"I'm really sorry about that night in New York," she said, breaking the silence.

"What do you mean?"

"I didn't want the champagne to go to waste, and I think I got a little tipsy and handsy with your--" she stopped talking and motioned to my arms.

I wasn't sure if it was just the hot water or if she was blushing looking at my biceps."My what?" I asked.

Betty let out a nervous giggle. "You know."

Now this was getting interesting. Why was Betty getting so shy? Could Betty be thinking about me like I've been thinking about her?

I couldn't resist and teased her some more. "My biceps? How hard and big they are?"

Her jaw dropped open, and she buried her face in her hand. "I hoped you'd forgotten that."

Teasing her wasn't right, but it was so much fun. "I'd never forget that. Every guy dreams of hearing it."

She blushed, and I could see her breathing had sped up. I loved watching her squirm.

"Please," she begged. "I'm mortified here."

Okay, enough was enough. I worried I'd taken it too far.

"Betty," I said, wanting to put her at ease.

She took her hand away from face and looked over at me. Our eyes locked.

With her flushed cheeks, wet body, and slightly parted lips, my mind conjured up the image of her underneath me.

"Yes?" she asked, interrupting my thoughts.

"Don't worry. It's fine," I said, my voice came out lower and more gravelly than I intended.

"If it's fine now, does this mean you'll stop avoiding me?"

"We see each other all the time."

"Only when the kids are around," she said. "The second they go to bed, you hide in your room."

"I just wanted to give you your time off."

She folded her arms and raised her eyebrows. "Baloney. You're avoiding me and it's hurting my feelings. Am I going to be out of a job in a month?"

Oh Shit! I hadn't realized that taking a step back would bother Betty, and I certainly didn't want her to think that her job was in jeopardy.

"Betty, I'm sorry. I was trying to give you space and not act like some creepy boss trying to take advantage of his young nanny."

"I'm not that young," she interrupted. "We're probably only five or six years apart in age."

"You're like twenty years old --"

"I'm twenty-eight, and I'll be twenty-nine in March."

I laughed. "Betty, that's five months away. And I'll be thirty-eight in April."

"Ten years isn't that long of a time, and none of it is a good reason for you to avoid me. I love talking to the kids all day, but it would be nice to have a grownup conversation every once in a while."

"As I was saying, I'm sorry. I was wrong. You're right. We should talk more. Just let me know when you need to have some alone time."

She smiled. "It's a deal."

We both sat in the water, just smiling at each other. And then, out of nowhere, Betty splashed me.

I got a mouthful of hot tub water, which made her laugh.

"So it's like that, is it?" I said, standing up to get closer to counterattack.

She let out a shriek as she tried to scramble away from me. "Oh yeah. It's like that!"

I splashed her back and got her right in the face. She laughed as she choked on the water.

She was adorable. It would be nice to be friends. Sure, there was an attraction. But that was natural. I could keep it under control.

As she jumped up to splash me again, I caught a peek of her bush sticking out of the side of her bikini bottoms. I fought back a groan and pushed away the vision of me tearing those bottoms off and her legs over my shoulders.

While I was distracted, she got me right in the face with another splash.

"Take that!" she yelled.

Even though it'd be tough, I'd keep it friendly, yet professional for the kids' sake.

But first, I'd win this splash fight. After all, she started it.

36

BETTY

I headed to the kitchen to see how much longer it would be for dinner. The kids were changing into their clothes and tidying their rooms.

Over the last few weeks since Tyler and I had the talk in the hot tub, the family settled into a fun routine.

I'd wake up with the kids, and get them ready while Tyler showered and got dressed. Then he'd make breakfast while I got ready. We'd eat breakfast together as a family, and he'd head to the office. Most afternoons he'd video call the kids when Riley got home from school.

Chef Jerome prepared dinner and the next day's lunches each night. I'd eat dinner with the kids. Tyler would be home in time to put them to bed most of the days, and afterwards he'd work out.

Then, before bed, Tyler and I would sit out on the deck next to the heat lamp and enjoy hot chocolate together. Well, mine was hot chocolate. His was some sort of weird heated chocolate protein powder.

The kids were all cleaned up and spending a few minutes in the playroom before dinner. When I got to the dining room, I found Chef Jerome setting the table for four.

"Did I mix up the night that Uncle M's stopping by for dinner?" I asked.

"Mr. Tyler telephoned while you were in the bath with the children. He said he'd be home for dinner."

I whipped out my phone, and I saw a text from him. I hearted it. "That's great! I wanted to talk to him about Halloween costumes for the kids. Things must be going better at work because he's been coming home more often."

Chef Jerome paused from setting the table and looked up at me with a little smirk. "It's the third time this week. It's becoming a habit."

"What?" I asked.

"Nothing," he said, heading back into the kitchen.

I followed him. "That 'nothing' is the biggest something that I've ever seen or heard."

"It's none of my business, and I could be wrong."

Chef Jerome was 5 foot five, but his confidence gave him the aura of a man 6 foot ten. He never listened to critics, and he never felt like he was wrong.

"Tell me what's going on in there," I said, pointing to his brain.

"You really don't see it, do you?"

I looked down at my shirt to see if there was some

sort of stain from playing with the kids. Clothing stains run rampant in my life as a nanny.

"Oh my God!" Jerome said. "There really isn't anything going on between you two."

My mouth dropped open, and I realized Jerome was talking about me and Tyler. "Of course not! He's my boss. And he's a good boss, and I'm an excellent employee."

"No, no, no, honey," Jerome said. "I meant nothing bad. I just thought there was a little chemistry between the two of you. Honestly, I think you two would be great together."

"No," I said. "There's nothing between Tyler and me. It's just nice to have a boss that appreciates my hard work."

"He appreciates more than your hard work."

"There's nothing going on," I said, my heart beating in my chest.

If Jerome sensed I had a big crush on Tyler, did Tyler notice?

But inside, my mind bubbled with way too many thoughts. Could there ever be something between us? Did I want that? Did he want that?

The sound of the front door opening interrupted my thoughts.

I told myself to act like everything was fine, even though nothing about my mental state was fine.

37

TYLER

At my desk, I stared at the choices of Halloween costumes that Betty and the kids picked out. They were all super cute, but one really stood out to me. It was the costume the kids wanted the most -- the Peter Pan themed one.

The only catch was that it was a four-person costume. The kids wanted to go as Peter Pan and Tinker Bell, and they wanted me to be Captain Hook with Betty going as Wendy.

The Halloween party fell on a Saturday, but Betty said she wouldn't mind going. She'd already spent her last few Saturdays hanging out with the family.

I've been paying her overtime, but she insisted that she go to the Halloween party with us just for fun.

She'd even offered to alter the Captain Hook costume so it would fit me, but I told her I'd have my tailor do it.

Someone knocked on my office door, and then just

walked right in. I looked up. It was Nick. I should've known by the way he waltzed in here, like he owned the place. Although, being our very first investor, my brother-in-law did own a lot of the place.

"Have you thought about what you're doing for Thanksgiving?" Nick asked.

"I haven't even figured out our costumes for your dad's party next weekend," I said, motioning to the myriad of Halloween printouts the kids had given me.

Nick looked down at the papers.

"That bee costume looks really cute, and every girl loves being a princess. But what's this?"

Nick pointed to the Peter Pan foursome. "Is Mr. I Don't Participate in Anything actually considering dressing up this year?"

"The kids want me to be Captain Hook and they want Betty to be Wendy."

"That's perfect. What's the problem?"

"I can't have Betty work on a holiday. She's already spent some of her days off with us."

"You can always ask her. She may want the overtime."

"Oh, she's all for it. She just won't let me pay her."

Nick sat down on my sofa. "And why is that a problem?"

He was smiling.

"What are you grinning about?" I asked.

"You know you've been talking about her nonstop for a month now."

"The kids are very fond of her."

"I think she's great. So does Meredith."

"You've never met her," I said.

"I saw you two in that viral video. Very cute stuff. The entire internet agrees with me. Let her go with you on Halloween and bring her by on Thanksgiving."

"You mean have her work every single holiday?" I said. "And everybody calls me the heartless one."

"I wasn't suggesting she come by for Thanksgiving to work. I was suggesting she come as your date."

"Are you fucking crazy?"

"Meredith says you two are perfect together, and your cousin and his wife are bringing their twins. So we'll have a babysitter there to look after the kids. Betty can just sit back and relax."

"I don't think it's a good idea," I said, wondering if Betty would even say yes to something like that.

Nick stood up. "Well, we'll see what Betty has to say. Because Meredith is inviting her to Thanksgiving."

"Don't you dare!" I said.

"I didn't think you'd be mad, and there's always a chance she'll say no. But there's no stopping it. Meredith already emailed invitations. Yours is the one that hasn't been opened, so she sent me here to ask if you're coming. We've got a big announcement."

"How big? Like something that would turn out to be around 8 pounds 3 ounces?"

"RSVP to Thanksgiving, and don't say a word about our big announcement to anyone. Especially not Meredith."

Nick left my office, and I sat there dumbfounded.

My stomach was doing somersaults thinking about dinner with Betty tonight. The major problem was that I couldn't decide which answer I feared more--her saying yes or her saying no.

38

BETTY

My entire body trembled with anxiety. I thought we were going to a simple kids' Halloween party, but it was a giant bash in Beverly Hills with super rich people and celebrities.

It was at the super famous pop singer, Angela Debeers's, house. M-Forty and Angela were all over the tabloids. They'd gone through a breakup in the nineties, and they'd been dating under the radar for the last couple of years.

But the paparazzi had gotten wind of their rekindled romance and started following them around again. I'd read about this party on a celebrity gossip site.

Apparently, tons of celebrities and their kids were going to this party. I wanted to crawl under the covers and fake being ill, but the kids really were excited about our family costume. The party just seemed way to upscale for me. I felt like everyone there would know that I didn't belong, or worse, treat me like a charity case.

I figured I would make an appearance and then duck out early. It was my night off, after all.

I checked my watch, and it was 6:30. Time to face the music. I went to the kids' rooms to make sure they hadn't destroyed their costumes in the ten minutes that it took me to get ready.

I ran into Tyler in the hallway. How did he make a Captain Hook costume look sexy? The tailor had done a great job. He practically rebuilt the entire costume from scratch to make it fit Tyler. We entered the playroom, where I'd left the kids to get ready, and thankfully, their costumes were still intact.

"Daddy!" Riley said. "You look just like the book."

Tyler bent down and showed the kids his hook. "Aargh! I'm not Daddy. I'm the ferocious Captain Hook, and if you're not good tonight, I'll make you walk the plank."

Then he tickled both the kids, and they exploded into fits of laughter.

"You can't make me walk the plank," Riley said. "I can fly."

Renzo jumped up. "I can fly, too!"

"I guess that just leaves me to walk the plank," I said.

Tyler's brown eyes swept over my body, and then he gave me a flirty smile. "Or I'll just keep Wendy as my prisoner."

I know he was just teasing, but my knees felt like

they were going to buckle. How the hell was I going to get through this night?

He looked me up and down and smiled. "Looks like Wendy is all grown up."

"And Captain Hook has been stepping up his workouts," I said.

"Gotta keep in shape to plunder the most booty," he said with a wink.

I laughed out loud and played it cool, but inside I was dying. I'd been spending way too much time fantasizing about what life could be like if something happened between me and Tyler.

39

TYLER

Betty hadn't said a word about Thanksgiving to me, and I was determined to find out if she'd intended to go. Things between us had gotten a little flirty, and, as far as I could tell, she didn't mind.

I toyed with the idea of asking her to be my date at Thanksgiving to make sure that she knew she wasn't working. She looked adorable in her floor-length, light blue Wendy dress, and looking at our family dressed up together made my heart fill with contentment.

Somehow, with Betty here, we really felt like a family.

Our driver pulled up to the front gate of Angela's house. There was a giant skeleton that actually moved, a pumpkin patch, and a giant haunted house.

The kids squealed and pointed at every single thing and were practically jumping up and down in their seats.

I looked over at Betty. She looked terrified.

"Are you okay?" I asked.

"Just a little nervous."

I reached over and squeezed her hand to comfort her, and she squeezed mine back. "It'll be fun," I said.

She nodded, squeezed my hand some more, and didn't let go. I stared out the window, grateful that there was a long line of cars ahead of us going up to the house. Holding Betty's hand felt so good, I wasn't ready for it to end.

When we finally exited the car to enter the party, Betty took Riley's hand, and I took Renzo's hand. I could see she was still nervous, so I grabbed Betty's free hand and we entered the party as a family. I leaned over and whispered in her ear. "Don't worry about a thing. I'm right here."

I understood what it felt like to be intimidated by parties like this. My friends and I had attended them when I was growing up, but my family was not as well-off as the kids in my private school.

I vowed to keep Betty by my side. Mick came up to us with a hot brunette. He was wearing a black wig with ugly bangs, and then a moment later I put it together.

The brunette was Angela, and the two of them had dressed as Sonny and Cher.

"I'm so glad you made it! What a great costume!" Mick said, motioning to us.

"Likewise," I said.

"Uncle M!" Renzo shouted.

"I'm Angela," Angela said, reaching out to shake Betty's hand.

Betty shook her hand and introduced herself, and the two of them made small talk.

"There are activities outside for the kids. If you want, I'll bring them there," M-Forty said. "There's staff out there to make sure all the kids are safe, so the grown-ups can have fun at the party, too."

"I can take the children," Betty said.

"No," M-Forty said, taking the children by the hand and shooing Betty away. "We invited you as a guest. No working for you."

"I better make my rounds with the other guests. I'm a little nervous," Angela said. "Somebody told me Cher might stop by."

"She'll get a kick out of it," M-Forty said. "Now, are you guys ready for some candy and a haunted house?"

"Candy!" Renzo yelled.

"Can we?" Riley asked, looking up at me.

"All right. But not too much candy. You don't want to get sick."

But the kids didn't sound like they were listening to my warnings as they ran off with their uncle.

Meredith and Nick waved and came over. They'd dressed as Fred and Wilma Flintstone.

"Love your costumes," Meredith said.

"Betty and the kids picked it out," I said.

"They're Tinker Bell and Peter Pan," Betty explained. "You two look great."

"We saw the kids. They looked adorable," Nick said.

"Wait! I don't think the two of you have met," Meredith said. "This is my husband, Nick."

"Uncle M's my dad," Nick said, shaking Betty's hand. "It's so great to meet you. Tyler never stops talking about you."

I was going to kill him for that.

"Meredith!" my cousin-in-law, Lauren, yelled from across the room. "There you are!"

"That's Lauren," Meredith said to Betty. "I just have to introduce you."

And before I could stop her, my sister whisked Betty away. Shit. So much for sticking by Betty's side.

"You two look pretty cozy," Nick said as they got out of earshot.

"There's nothing going on between us," I said, but a part of me wished there was, even though I didn't say it out loud.

"She hasn't responded to our Thanksgiving invitation, but I imagine Meredith will take care of that right now. So what's the deal? I know you're into her."

"It's a tricky situation. She is amazing with the kids, and I can't risk losing the only nanny the kids have ever gotten along with."

"That's one way to look at it," Nick said. "You might fall in love and stay together forever."

"Did you really just say that?" I asked.

"Yes, I did, and I don't feel ashamed about it for one minute. Love has made me a romantic, and it'll do the same for you."

I glanced across the room and watched Meredith

introduce Betty to Lauren, Carolyn, and Mackenzie-- the three women who married my cousins.

Several men were ogling the group of women. The five of them together made quite the attractive pack.

"Easy there, tiger," Nick said. "The ladies know how to protect each other."

Easy for him to say. He was married, but the situation between Betty and me was more vague. The last thing I needed was some random dude to step in and confuse the situation even more.

I continued to keep an eye on Betty. She was smiling, but it was her polite smile. She wasn't having a good time.

I needed to get over there, but some friends of mine from school waylaid me. We talked about the business and traffic, and when I looked back over at the group of women, Betty wasn't there.

My gut dropped. If she left the group, she probably wasn't having a good time. I felt like I'd let her down.

40

BETTY

Meredith introduced me to her friends. It turns out they were all bridesmaids at each other's weddings.

Their friendliness overwhelmed me. I was used to spending time with small toddlers, and being around grown-ups in such a luxury setting made me feel self-conscious.

When Meredith introduced me to Mackenzie, I almost couldn't speak. I'd listened to Mackie B's songs on the radio all the time. I didn't know whether I should say anything about it, and the moment passed.

We made small talk for a little while, and I learned that the three women had married Meredith's cousins.

"So enough small talk," Meredith said. "Are you and Tyler an item yet?"

"You two look great together," Mackie added.

They all stared. My face flushed with embarrassment. Could everyone see my big crush on Tyler? I didn't belong here. My heart beat in my throat. "I'm just the nanny. He's a really great boss."

Meredith nodded and looked at her friends.

"What?" I asked.

Carolyn, the curvy blonde, piped in. "Sometimes when you fall in love, you're the last one to admit it. Trust me. I've been there."

"Me, too," Lauren said. "And Aiden, my husband, was my boss as well. Very tricky."

"Not nearly as tricky as faking being a couple and then actually becoming a couple," Mackie said.

"Hello, my situation with Nick wasn't easy either," Meredith said. "He was my brother's best friend, and he hated me. You two will work this out."

"I really appreciate all your encouragement, but I'm just the nanny," I said, wishing the conversation would end.

"Sorry," Carolyn said, sensing that I felt uncomfortable.

"We're just glad to meet someone new. All these rich people made me nervous when I started hanging around the Bronsons," Lauren said.

"I grew up around these people, and I never felt like I belonged," Meredith confessed. "When these three married into the family, I finally felt like I had someone in the family I could relate to. I hope we can be friends."

"That's really cool of you guys. Sounds great," I said, needing to get the hell out of here. I knew they meant well, but everyone talking about Tyler and me being a couple, and how I wasn't rich, was everything I'd wanted to avoid tonight. The attention, although kind hearted, overwhelmed me.

They might not have been rich before, but they certainly were now. I felt like I stuck out like a charity case.

"Can you point me to the bathroom?" I asked a passing waiter.

"I'll show you where it is," Meredith said, but I waved her off.

I needed to find Tyler and tell him I wasn't feeling well so I could go home. Coming to this party was a big mistake. I went to the bathroom because I felt like I had to commit to my excuse, and when I got out, I scanned the party for Tyler.

"Hey," a man dressed up as a wolf said to me. "I've never seen you at one of these before."

"I've never been at one of these before," I said.

"So are you, Belle?" he said, motioning to my costume.

"No, I'm Wendy from Peter Pan. Close though. And are you a werewolf?" I asked.

"Nope. I'm the Big Bad Wolf," he said, waggling his eyes.

I laughed.

"Let's get you a drink," he said.

"Actually, I'm not feeling well. I think I'm going to head home. Have you seen Tyler Bronson?"

"My cousin, Tyler? Yeah, just a few minutes ago. I know he's around here somewhere. Are you his date?"

THE NEW SINGLE DAD BILLIONAIRE

A frustrated sigh escaped from my mouth before I could stop it. "No, I'm just the nanny."

"So you didn't come here with a date?" he asked, waggling his eyebrows again.

I laughed. Well, at least I knew what his intentions were.

"I should get home," I said.

"The party just started, and these things are always awkward in the beginning. Have one drink, and if you're not happy, I'll have my driver take you home, and I'll let Tyler know. Okay?"

I shook my head no. "You're a total stranger, and I don't even know your name. I'm definitely not getting in some random car. Stranger Danger."

The man laughed. "Yeah, of course. I'm so used to everyone here knowing each other. I'm Miles. Listen, it'll look better if you stick around just a little while. It'll make the host and Tyler feel less concerned for you."

He had a point. I didn't want to be rude.

"Okay, where is the bar?" I asked.

He held out his arm for me. I took it, and he led the way.

41

TYLER

I needed to find Betty, but I kept getting stopped by people to talk. Where was she?

I ran into Lauren and Aiden, my cousin. "Have either of you seen Betty lately?"

"She went to the bathroom a little while ago, but I haven't seen her since."

"Which one is Betty?" Aiden asked.

"She's dressed as Wendy to go with our Peter Pan theme."

"Was she wearing a long blue dress with like a bow in her hair?" Aiden asked.

"That's her," I said.

"I saw her at the bar near the grand piano about fifteen minutes ago with Miles."

My fists clenched, but I tried to hide my temper. My cousin Miles was a fun guy, but he had a reputation with the ladies. There was no fucking way I wanted him talking to Betty.

I pushed my way to the crowd to get to the bar, but I didn't see them.

People tried to talk to me, but I ignored them. Finally, I spotted them along the wall right near the front foyer. My cousin was dressed as a wolf. That's for damn sure.

"Betty!" I said, deliberately standing very close to Miles. He had his arm up against the wall, leaning way too close to Betty.

Miles looked over, and he knew what he was doing.

"Your nanny was just telling me about what a horrible boss you are," he said.

Betty gave him a playful slap on the shoulder. "I was not."

I knew Betty was a lightweight with drinking, and there was no fucking way I was gonna let Miles take advantage of her. What's that you got there?" I asked, waving to her drink.

"I didn't know what to order, so Miles suggested I get the Long Island Iced Tea. It tastes good."

I glared at my cousin. Seriously! A fucking Long Island Iced Tea.

"Those are pretty strong. Are you feeling okay?" I asked.

"She's fine," Miles said. "Don't worry. I'll take care of her for you."

I ignored my cousin.

"Actually," Betty said. "I'm feeling a little light-headed. Maybe it's best that I go home."

"Yes, I'll let M-Forty know that I'm taking you home, and I'll come back for the kids."

"Nonsense," Miles said. "No point in you going all the way home and then back here. I'm staying in Malibu, and I've got an early flight. How about I take Betty home for you?"

"That's okay," I said, taking Betty by the arm and leading her out the front door.

Miles followed us outside. "I'll wait here with her to make sure she's okay, while you talk to M-Forty about the kids."

"It's fine," Betty said. "I hate to create a fuss. I just want to call an Uber and crawl into bed."

"Betty, I've got the driver for the night. Richard will take you home," I said. "I just don't want you to be alone."

"Well, if that's the case --" Miles started.

I turned to him, and didn't hide my anger. "Miles," I said through gritted teeth.

He took a step back, but I stepped forward, getting very close to him. If he didn't back off, I was going to make him back off.

He took another step back, not realizing he was stepping off the curb. His leg bent into an awkward position as he lost his footing. His shoulder and entire side thudded hard against the driveway. Brakes screeched.

"Miles!" Betty yelled as she ran to see if he was okay. Everyone gathered around and stared at me like I'd punched him.

42

BETTY

Tyler had insisted I have today off, and now I was glad he had. My plan was to hide out in my room. Last night had been an utter disaster.

Miles left the party with what I hoped was only a broken ankle. In the end, our driver for the night took me home, and Tyler stayed with the kids at the party at my insistence. He hadn't seemed happy about it at all.

I know he didn't feel great about things. I sat on the sofa in my room and stared out the large window. My room faced the side of the house with a view of the garden. The beautiful view barely registered in my mind.

What was going on between Tyler and me? He seemed jealous last night, and a part of me liked it until all the commotion.

The sound of little feet thumped down the hallway, followed by a light, erratic knock. It was probably Renzo.

I went over and opened the door. Yup, Renzo.

"Daddy wanted me to ask you if you wanted to have waffles with us?"

So he sent the kid instead of coming himself. Interesting.

"I'm not feeling very well. I might just go to bed."

Renzo grabbed my hand and tugged at it. "Waffles make you better."

His adorable face was impossible to resist. Besides, maybe it would be good to see what Tyler had to say for himself.

I entered the kitchen, and Riley looked up. She was seated on a bar stool near the kitchen island. Tyler stood next to her, manning the waffle iron.

"Betty! Did you see what I got?" Riley asked, tugging on the Hawaiian lei that she must've gotten at the party. "It's a flower necklace. I got a matching crown for it, but I lost it."

"Did you guys have fun at the party?" I asked the kids.

"We got candy!" Renzo said.

"Dad says we can only eat a couple of pieces at a time to make it last," Riley said.

I looked over at Tyler. He avoided my gaze and focused on the waffle maker. "Did your dad say anything else about the party last night?"

"No," Riley said.

"Here you go, Riley-roo," Tyler said, handing her a waffle on a plastic plate.

"And here's yours," he said to Renzo.

THE NEW SINGLE DAD BILLIONAIRE

"Yours will be ready in a jiffy," Tyler said, looking at me.

I poured juice for the kids and grabbed myself a cup of coffee. We ate breakfast as close to normal as possible, but Tyler and I mostly spoke to the kids.

When we loaded the dishes into the dishwasher, Tyler sent the kids to play in their room and asked to talk to me.

"About last night," he said.

"Yes, what happened there?"

"My cousin Miles is a fun guy, but he wasn't just dressed as the Big Bad Wolf. He is a wolf."

"Maybe I was in the mood for a wolf," I said. If Tyler wouldn't fess up to being jealous, then I would't fess up about anything either.

"You're not the to go home with the wolf type, Betty."

I didn't like the way this conversation was going, and I didn't like what he was implying. "Women can go home with someone and not be considered a certain type. I can be a nice person and good at my job, and go home with men I meet at a party if I want to."

"You wanted to go home with him?" Tyler asked, his nostrils flaring.

I put my hands on my hips. "Why is that any of your business?"

"You damn well know why."

"Actually, I don't, Tyler. What exactly is going on here?"

"I'm trying to protect you from fucking wolves, and you don't seem to care," he growled back.

"Really?" I asked. "Because you seem kinda jealous, and it looked like if he hadn't fallen over, you were going to kill that guy."

"He was trying to get you drunk and take advantage of you. Do you think I'd let him do that?"

"That's not what I'm talking about, and I can take care of myself."

"Then what are you talking about?" he asked.

I wasn't going to broach the subject. It was too embarrassing. I never should've never left my room." Forget it. I must've been mistaken."

I turned to leave, but Tyler grabbed my arm. "Mistaken about what, Betty?" He asked, his voice softer and gentler.

"Please, Tyler. I was embarrassed enough last night, and I don't feel like doing it again this morning."

He let go of my arm, and I walked away.

"Betty! Wait!" He said, rushing behind me. I stopped and turned back around, but I hadn't realized that he was so close. I smacked into his chest and stumbled backwards.

He caught me by my arms to keep me from falling. My arms wrapped around his waist in a panic, but once I was safe, I didn't let go. Neither did he. I looked up at him.

My gaze drifted to his lips. Please God, let Tyler Bronson kiss me.

43

TYLER

I don't know what came over me, but with the way she looked at me and the feel of her body in my arms, I went for it.

I pulled her closer, bent down, and gave her a gentle kiss on the lips. Her lips parted, and I dared to kiss her deeper. She responded by opening her mouth for me.

Our tongues swirled around each other, and I let my hand drift down to cup her ass. She moaned in my mouth, and she slid her hand under my shirt. The feeling of her bare hand against my skin made me rock hard.

"Daddy!" Renzo yelled. The two of us immediately stopped kissing and took a step back.

"Yes, son," I yelled back, turning to the hallway. I heard his footsteps come down the hall, and I was relieved that he hadn't caught us.

"Riley is sneaking candy, and she won't share with me."

I turned back to Betty.

"Would you mind handling that for me?" she asked. "I forgot something in my room."

"It's your day off, remember?" I said.

She was still breathing heavily from our kiss, and all I could think of was when could we do that again. And how much I wanted more.

"Somehow it slipped my mind," she said.

We both stood there, grinning at each other. I know how it slipped her mind.

"Daddy!" Renzo pleaded.

"Okay," I said.

I followed Renzo to deal with the candy situation, but as soon as the kids went to bed tonight, Betty and I were going to pick up where we left off.

44

BETTY

I jumped in the tub to get ready for dinner. Well, I was actually getting ready for when the kids went to bed. I wanted to shave my legs just in case things went further with Tyler and me.

We'd been stealing glances at each other all day, and I caught myself wanting to call someone. Except, I didn't really have anyone to call but Caitlyn.

I worried if I told her I would lose the magic of the moment, if she asked a bunch of questions about the future or the present.

Affairs between dads and nannies are rampant, but it rarely ends well.

But I didn't want to think about any of that. I only wanted to think about that kiss.

I've never had anyone kiss me like that, a toe-curling mixture of passion and tenderness. His brawny arms around my body, and then when he grabbed my ass and pulled me close.

Damn. It was like my insides morphed into molten lava.

I hurried to get ready for dinner, but I didn't know what to wear. It felt like I was getting ready for a date, but it was dinner with the family.

I looked into my closet. Well, it wasn't like I had anything date-like to wear, anyway. No wonder Caitlin had bought me that dress.

I settled on a low cut pink top with my good bra underneath and a pair of yoga pants. I looked good, but still casual. Or at least I hoped so.

I kept my hair down instead of wearing it in a ponytail, and I took extra time with my makeup.

Normally, I didn't wear makeup. But I wanted to look my best, while simultaneously avoiding looking like I was trying to look my best.

I heard little footsteps running down the hallway. It had to be Renzo calling for dinner.

I opened the door before Renzo knocked, and he looked up at me.

"Is it dinnertime?"

He nodded and just stood there, staring at me.

"Should we go to dinner?" I asked him.

He nodded again, and I took his hand and walked to the dining room with him.

When I got to the table, I lifted him up and put him in his booster seat. He put his hands in my hair and played with it. "Pretty."

"Thank you," I said to Renzo.

"Yeah, you look really pretty," Riley said.

"Yes, Betty really does," Tyler said, giving me a sexy smile. So much for not looking like I'd tried to dress up.

The smoldering look Tyler gave me made me stop breathing for a moment. I steadied myself by putting my hand on the table, forced myself to take a breath, and sat down.

This is going to be the longest dinner of my life.

45

TYLER

I put the dishes away and waited for Betty to return from reading the kids a story. She insisted on doing the bedtime stories, and it made Riley happy.

I only agreed because the two of us splitting the work made it faster to get the kids to bed, so we could be alone.

My cock twitched in my pants just thinking about it. The only catch is I didn't know how far she wanted to go. I'd settle for just a make-out session, but I wanted all of her. And I was prepared for anything and everything.

A tinge of worry niggled in the back of my brain, but I pushed it aside. I wanted this. Consequences be damned.

I heard the door to the kids' room shut. My knee-jerk reaction was to dash over, grab her, throw her on the couch, but I opted to walk out at a slow pace.

"They're asleep," she said as we met in the living room.

I smiled and took a step toward her. "Thanks for helping me."

"Of course," she said, but neither of us were really focused on the conversation.

I closed the distance between us, and she looked up at me with those green eyes. I brushed her long, dark brown hair out of her face.

"Did you wear your hair down for me?" I asked, my eyes fixed on hers.

"Did you wear that cologne just for me?"

"You better believe I did," I said, not hiding my need for her in my voice.

Her eyes widened, and her lips parted. Bingo.

I bent down and kissed her. It was just as good as this afternoon. We shared a deep kiss until one kid coughed.

We both stopped, and our heads snapped toward the kids' rooms. Was someone going to come out?

"I'll check on them really quick," I said, rushing down the hall.

Making sure not to make any noise, I cracked each of their doors open one by one to see if anyone was awake. Luckily, both of them were asleep. Thank God!

I rushed back to the living room and whispered to Betty. "Let's go out on the deck."

She nodded in agreement and the two of us tiptoed outside, holding hands. I felt like a giddy schoolboy, but I played it cool. No matter how far things went tonight, I would make sure that I'd rock Betty's world. She'd already rocked mine.

46

BETTY

One kiss and my panties were already wet. Holy smokes! I was glad we were going outside. I didn't want the kids to hear us, and I didn't want Tyler to see how much I was blushing.

It was chilly outside, and I expected Tyler to turn on one of the outdoor heat lamps where we usually sat. Instead, he led me over to the other side of the deck, where there was an outdoor fire pit.

I'd never been to this side of the deck before. It was just outside of Tyler's room, and I always viewed it as his private space. From what I could tell in the dark, this side of the deck had several chairs, a coffee table, and a side table.

Tyler bent over and lit a fire in the pit. It warmed the space and cast a romantic glow. That's when I spotted the ice bucket, glasses, and champagne.

"You seemed to respond well to champagne in New York, so..." he said.

"When did you have time to put this together?"

He pulled the bottle out of the ice. "I made a couple of calls."

I kept forgetting how rich he was.

"It's just like The Plaza, minus the chocolate-covered strawberries," I said.

"Do you think I'm an amateur?" He pointed to a silver covered tray on the little side table, and I opened it. There they were, along with even more fruit, and marshmallows and graham crackers to make s'mores.

"You thought of everything!"

"You don't know the half of it," he said, popping the champagne cork.

Seeing how Tyler had gone through so much trouble to make sure that we had a great time excited and worried me.

The sounds of the waves cresting onto the rocks on the beach below added to the romance of the night. I couldn't quite see the ocean, but I could make out tiny flicks of moonlight reflected on the water.

Like he said, he obviously wasn't an amateur, but I was. I'd only been with three men, and as much fun as I thought it would be, the sex wasn't as exciting as I'd hoped. I wondered if I was the problem.

But none of their kisses even came close to Tyler's. I worried I wasn't sexy enough for Tyler.

"Talk to me, Betty," Tyler said, kneeling in front of me like he did to the kids when he sensed they were distressed.

"I'm a little nervous."

He put his hand on my knee and smiled at me. "We don't have to do anything you don't want to do. There's no pressure."

"No! It's not that," I said, my voice coming out stronger than I intended.

He nodded and laughed. "Good to know."

"I just --" I turned away from Tyler, too embarrassed to continue.

"How about we just sit here for a second or two and enjoy each other's company?" Tyler suggested.

I nodded my head yes, and he handed me a glass of champagne. He took his glass, sat down next to me on the loveseat, and put his arm around me.

I took a deep breath in and relaxed, nuzzling my head into the crook of his arm. He cupped my shoulder, and I put my hand on his leg.

"This feels nice," he said.

"It does," I agreed.

I sipped my champagne with my free hand as Tyler stroked my shoulder.

I moved my hand higher on his leg, and I felt his chest move up and down just a little faster.

His hand drifted from my shoulder to my neck, and he stroked my ear with his finger. My entire body buzzed with excitement.

I finished my champagne, but I didn't want to spoil the mood by moving to set the empty glass on the table.

Between the heat from the fire and Tyler's body, the chill in the air had evaporated.

Tyler leaned forward, put his empty glass on the table, and took mine as well.

When he leaned back, he scooped me into his lap.

"This can't be comfortable for you," I said motioning to his lap.

"Comfortable isn't the word I'd use, but I definitely like it. Let's make it even more fun," he said, scooting us closer to the corner of the loveseat.

"Wait," I said, not wanting to worry about his legs going numb. I scooched back so that my butt was on the loveseat and my legs were over his lap. I rested my back on the arm of the chair.

He laughed. "Better?"

I nodded.

"This next part is cheesy, but it's happening, so stifle your inner cringe," he said.

"Okay," I said, nervous about what he was going to do next.

He reached over, grabbed a strawberry, and held it in front of my lips.

I giggled with the over-the-top ridiculousness of it.

"Open up, Betty," he said. "You don't want me to make airplane noises."

I humored him and opened my mouth to take a bite. But as he watched me with hungry eyes, I bit into the strawberry, and my insides melted.

I swallowed the strawberry, and a bit of juice dribbled down my mouth. I felt self-conscious, but he wiped it away with his finger.

"Was it good?" he asked, his voice a sexy whisper.

I couldn't even talk, so I just nodded yes.

He smiled and kissed me. The taste of his tongue, along with the leftover strawberry, was incredible.

A moan escaped from my throat. He kissed me deeper.

He shifted his body weight, and his erection grazed against my leg.

He groaned, and his hand slipped under my shirt. My heart beat even faster, and my breathing sped up.

"God, you feel so good," he said, taking a breath from our kisses and then diving back in for more.

His dizzying kisses made me even more wet, and I ran my hand along his chest to feel his hard body.

His hand moved up my torso and under my bra. I gasped as he tweaked my nipple. He groaned as he continued to kiss me.

After a few minutes, Tyler took his hand out from under my shirt, and reached under my legs. I didn't know what he was doing, but somehow, a few seconds later, I was lying on my back on the loveseat with Tyler above me.

We kissed more and writhed against each other. I could feel his erection through my yoga pants. I bucked my hips to feel his hardness right on my sweet spot.

Tyler pushed up my shirt and bra exposing my breasts. Half a breath later, he went from kissing my lips to sucking my nipple.

"Oh my God! Tyler!" I said, my voice surprised and excited. I was this close to hitting my peak, but I didn't know if this was what I wanted at this moment.

I wanted more.

I pushed him away. He stopped and gave me a questioning look.

"I was about to--" I said, not finishing my sentence. I didn't know how to say what I meant.

He smiled and looked down at me. "I know. That was the idea."

"Oh."

Tyler's eyelids were at half-mast, and he went back to tweaking my nipple with his finger. "Did you want to finish in my bedroom?"

"Yes," I gasped.

Almost before I could finish saying yes, Tyler had whisked me into his arms and was opening up the sliding glass doors that led to his bedroom.

This was really happening!

47

TYLER

When she stopped me from finishing her, I thought she wanted to take a breather or call it a night.

But when I saw that look in her eye, I sensed she wanted to go further. The moment she said she wanted to finish things off in my bedroom, it was game on.

I hadn't been with anybody since the kids, and I'd never wanted anyone as bad as I wanted Betty.

Just the feeling of her legs wriggling across my cock almost made me come, but if she put my cock in her mouth I'd finish too soon.

Betty deserved a great time, and the idea of having to sit across the breakfast table from her knowing that I didn't satisfy her was not an option.

I'd left my bedroom lights on low in the one in a million chance we'd end up here. It pays to be prepared.

I set her on the bed, climbed in next to her, and

immediately lifted off her shirt. Looking over at her, chest heaving with excitement, her lips swollen from my kisses, my cocked throbbed in my pants.

She licked her lips and reached for my belt. Holy fuck! I reached behind her and undid her bra. She unzipped her pants and then took her hands away to remove her bra straps.

My pants practically strangled my cock, so I kicked off my shoes and tore them off.

Betty kicked her shoes off as well. I needed to get those pants off of her, but she seemed to have other ideas. Her hands reached for the bottom of my shirt, but there was no way she would be able to reach up high enough to get it off.

I took the hint, tore off my shirt, and looked down at her.

Seeing her breathless with her eyes roaming my entire body made me feel alive. Her gaze drifted down to the tent in my boxers.

Her eyes widened, and I let out a pleased chuckle. Her tiny hand pressed against my abs and then slowly drifted downward. I threw my head back and groaned.

Her hands were so soft, and her shy touch drove me crazy. I wanted to feel her hands wrapped around my cock, but the delicious agony of her slow, tentative strokes drove me insane in the best way.

When her tiny fingers finally reached my shaft, I hissed with excitement. "Betty."

Her touch went from tentative to more aggressive

THE NEW SINGLE DAD BILLIONAIRE

as she wrapped her hand around my dick and stroked me up and down.

Oh, hell no! That felt way too good. I reached down, grabbed her hand, and guided her to lie back on the bed.

I bent down, put my hands around the waistband of her yoga pants, and pulled them and her undies off in one swift motion.

She covered herself self-consciously, and I stopped her. "No. You're perfect, and I want to see every fucking inch of you."

Our eyes locked, and she put her hands up by her head. I took a moment to drink in the sight of her.

I realized I was still wearing my boxers, so I got out of the bed and pulled them off.

Her eyes were fixed on my cock, and I let her get a good look at me. I was proud of my body, and I loved the idea that it turned her on to see me.

I reached into my nightstand, grabbed a condom, and placed it on top of the nightstand so it would be at the ready. I wanted her to know that I'd be safe, and also to let her know I intended to fuck her.

If she wasn't interested, she could speak up.

I climbed into bed next to her. She turned to face me. I kissed her, and we stroked each other. I loved the feeling of our bodies rubbing up against each other. She kissed my neck and then down my chest, and I knew what she was trying to do.

But there was no way she was going to put my cock in her mouth and I wouldn't blow instantly. I wanted to make this last. We could save that for the second round.

I maneuvered my body between her legs and distracted her with more deep kisses. Feeling her soft skin underneath me felt like a dream. I'd been jacking off to her ever since I saw her in that see-through dress. And now she was here in my bed.

This was real--not a fucking fantasy. This was her flesh against mine.

I came up for breath. My hot breath on her ear.

"God, Tyler!" she whispered, almost as if she was saying it to herself.

My dick twitched at the sound of her voice saying my name. It was almost as if my cock knew she was calling for him.

"That's right," I growled into her ear. "Say my name. Tell me you want me, Betty."

She let out a sharp exhale and then, in a breathy voice, she said, "Tyler, I want you."

"Fuck yeah," I said.

I kissed her neck and sucked her nipple until she was writhing underneath me. Then I scooted down between her legs, putting her legs over my shoulders.

She closed her eyes.

"Betty," I said, my mouth inches from her hot slit.

I wanted to freeze this moment in my memory forever. The way her chin bunched up looking down at me. Her smell. Her gorgeous fucking bush. All of it.

Her gaze met mine. We locked eyes as I took my first taste of her sweet pussy.

Her hips bucked, and she hissed out, "Tyler!"

Her clit was so sensitive and swollen. I eased up the pressure. She ground herself into my mouth.

After a few minutes, I pulled back her lips and took my mouth away so I could admire her. I rubbed her clit with my thumb as her hips bucked.

"Tyler," she panted.

"What's that, Betty?"

Her chest heaved. "So, close."

I rubbed her clit some more with my thumb and slipped my index finger inside of her. Holy fuck! She was so fucking tight and wet.

Her eyes involuntarily closed, and I didn't stop her. She looked amazing, writhing under my touch. I didn't want her to come too fast. I wanted her to enjoy it, and get the buildup.

She was so sexy. I could spend all night just doing this. Looking up at her body, watching the sexy way she moved. All of it made me drunk with a joyous type of lust that I'd never felt before.

Then I realized. I was falling in love with Betty. Hell, not falling, fell.

I took my thumb away and replaced it with my mouth. As I licked her clit with increasing intensity, I curved the finger inside of her to hit that special spot.

Her legs tightened around me, and she bucked her hips more wildly.

"Oh my God! Tyler!" she said, her voice urgent.

I sucked her more and stroked her G spot with my finger. Her hands flew to my head as she tensed all over. I kept the exact intensity and pace so as to not throw off her concentration. I could tell she was climbing up to that peak.

Her pussy twitched around my finger.

"Tyler!" she yelled. "God, Tyler!"

Her legs shook, and she tried to pull away. I lightened the intensity of my tongue on her clit and slowed the pace and pressure of my finger inside of her. I wanted her to ride the wave of this orgasm for as long as she could.

"Oh, God!"

As the wave crested, I slowly slipped my finger outside of her, scooted my body next to hers, and wrapped my arms around her.

She shook against me. My chest filled with pride. I'd made her come so fucking hard, and all I could think of was doing it again.

The sound of a door shutting jolted me out of my afterglow.

Betty and I instinctively pulled apart from each other, our eyes open wide.

Had we woken up one of the kids?

48

BETTY

I hid under the covers, mortified. Tyler had thrown on his sweatpants and dashed out of the room to check on the kids.

I hadn't meant to be that loud. It never even occurred to me I could be loud. The other times I've had sex, I had to sort of force myself to make noises to get my partner to do the things I liked. Not that it worked.

But everything with Tyler worked. I'd enjoyed sex before, but now I understood what all the hype was about.

Tyler came back into the room.

"Is everything okay?" I asked, wincing.

"Everything's fine," he said. "Riley just got up to go to the bathroom. She's back in bed asleep."

"Thank God," I said. "I'm normally not like that."

Tyler smiled at me. "You will be with me."

A wave of giddiness crashed over me. I couldn't

even look him in the eye. Every single word he said to me made me want to squeal. This couldn't be real.

He crossed the room, peeled off his sweatpants, and joined me in the bed.

"Were you hiding under the covers, Betty?"

"Do you blame me?"

Tyler laughed. "This time, I'll remember to keep you quiet." And with that, he scooted closer, grabbed his arms around me, and pulled me against him.

I realized he hadn't come yet. I worried I wouldn't do as good a job as he did, but I'd give it my all.

I stroked him as he kissed me. He moaned in my mouth, and when we took a moment to catch our breath, I kissed his chest and worked my way downward. He stopped me as I reached his stomach.

I looked up at him with a questioning face.

"That's not what I'm looking for right now," he said.

"And what are you looking for?" I asked.

He rolled over on top of me, looked into my eyes with a smoldering intensity that I'd never seen in my life. He said, "I want to fuck you, Betty."

My mouth dropped open. I never had a man talk to me so directly before, and I couldn't believe how hot it was.

"Are you okay with that?" he asked, reaching for the condom on the nightstand.

Still stunned, I nodded yes.

"I want to hear you say it, Betty. Tell me what you want me to do."

I stared at him. He got up on his knees in the bed, opened the condom package, and slid it on.

What I said about his biceps was true for him down there. So hard. So big.

He positioned himself in between my legs, still on his knees. Looking up at his massive body, I felt dainty and small.

"Tell me, Betty. Tell me what you want me to do to you."

Staring at his muscular body, unlocked a desperate hunger that had been building inside me since that first night when he carried me out of the pool. "I want you to fuck me, Tyler. I want you to fuck me right now."

He groaned.

I rarely used foul language, but it thrilled me to see how my dirty talk had excited him.

Tyler leaned down and kissed me. I wrapped my legs around him, and he positioned himself at my entrance.

This was it. He locked eyes with me as he slid into me.

I gasped.

"Fuck, Betty, you feel so good," he said, his hot breath on my ear.

Hearing his excitement spurred me on. I wanted him to feel as good as he made me feel.

I clenched down on him and squeezed, and I heard him groan again. "Fuck."

He pistoned in and out of me, and I bucked my hips to meet his thrusts.

"So damn tight," he hissed.

He paused for a moment, and I knew what he was trying to do, but I wanted him to come hard like I had.

I wrapped my legs even tighter around his waist, pulled him deep inside me, thrusting my hips up to keep up the pace.

"Baby, if you keep doing that --"

"I want it. I want you to come for me, Tyler," I said, without an ounce of shyness.

He reared up onto his knees, grabbed my ankles with each of his hands, and spread my legs wide open. Oh my God!

He thrust deep inside me, faster and faster. I could feel him tensing as his breath quickened.

"Betty," he said, his voice an urgent whisper.

"Yes, Tyler. Come for me!" I demanded, my voice husky and stern in a way that I'd never used before.

He pumped harder and faster until he roared in ecstasy. This was the best sex in my entire life.

Tyler held the base of the condom and gently pulled out of me.

"Be right back," he said as he got off the bed and walked to the bathroom.

I looked at his muscular ass, amazed that he and I were together now.

Or were we?

He came back into the bedroom, and I realized I had to pee. "My turn."

I looked down at the floor to grab my shirt, and Tyler interrupted me. "Stay naked."

THE NEW SINGLE DAD BILLIONAIRE

I told myself that he'd already seen everything, and it felt good to be so free with him. So I walked to the bathroom, totally naked. I peeked back, and he was checking out my ass.

He winked at me. When I returned to the bedroom and got back into the bed, he pulled me onto his chest and kissed the top of my head.

"Sorry I couldn't wait for you," he said.

"I'm not."

"I'll make it up to you in the next round."

Next round!

49

TYLER

All I wanted to do was go home early, but I had a full schedule at work. I needed to get my ass in gear so I could at least get home to have dinner with the kids and Betty.

My thoughts turned back to last night. The second round had been more tender than the first.

Everything about Betty turned me on. She was sexy and natural. We just gelled. Images of her naked next to me and underneath me replayed in my mind.

A knock on the door interrupted my daydreams. "Come in."

Meredith entered, carrying her tablet. "You know, you should have an assistant outside."

"We had that, remember? It didn't work out. Besides, people are too afraid to knock on my door, but they weren't too afraid to ask for an appointment with my assistant. This way fewer people bother me." I gave my sister a pointed look.

"I've been bothering you since the day I was born. It's never going to stop. I'm relentless."

I laughed. "All right, Miss Relentless. What crazy scheme do you need me to sign off on now?"

My sister stopped and looked at me. "You're in a good mood."

"It's fading fast," I said.

"It's Betty, isn't it?"

Was it that obvious? I didn't want to talk about it. Everything was too new and tender. I wanted to savor it and keep it to myself before the outside world got in.

"I'm not discussing anything about Betty," I said. "Don't even go there."

"She still hasn't responded to my Thanksgiving invitation."

Not wanting to discuss Betty, I changed the subject. "You're taking a big risk having a Thanksgiving party. You know Mom will be all over you trying control things and make it all about her."

"Nick and I sent her on a round-the-world luxury cruise. She'll be in the middle of the ocean when the party happens," Meredith said.

I laughed. "Lured her away with a vacation. Very clever."

She nodded and then sighed. "Well, seeing that you're in a good mood, I take it you weren't on the internet much this weekend."

I didn't like where this was going. "What now?"

Betty opened up her tablet, called up a page on the internet, and handed it to me.

There was a picture of me dressed as Captain Hook, glaring at my cousin Miles on the pavement. The headline read, "Tech Tycoon Gives Unknown Man Right Hook."

Jesus Christ.

50

BETTY

I left the kids in the playroom to check on dinner. It'd been so hard to concentrate today. I had spent the entire day thinking about Tyler and counting the hours until he came home.

When I saw Chef Jerome setting the table for four, my heart sped up with nervousness. I rushed into my room to get ready for dinner. Once again, I was confronted with my limited clothing selection.

I opted to just wear jeans and a T-shirt, but I jumped in the shower to wash my hair. If my outfit would not be great, at least my hair would look nice.

As I blow dried my hair, my phone dinged. It was a text message from Caitlyn: *I leave town and suddenly you're going to swanky parties and having men fight over you.*

I didn't know what she was talking about. I texted her back three question marks.

My phone rang. I debated letting it go to voicemail,

but then I remembered the Halloween party. My stomach churned.

"Are you talking about the Halloween party?" I asked, not even saying hello.

"Have you been under a rock all weekend? Your new boss is all over the Internet."

"I was busy with the kids," I said, not wanting to let her know what I was really doing.

"Spill it. What's going on with you and Tyler Bronson?"

"What do you mean?" I asked, not wanting to lie.

"This is the second time you've gone viral, and each time it looks very couple like."

My heart soared at the idea that Tyler and I look like a couple. "I already told you about the mingle event, and I went to that Halloween party thinking it was going to be your standard Halloween party, bobbing for apples and cotton balls turned into spiderwebs."

"You're trying to change the subject. So what's the story with the wolf?"

"Tyler didn't hit him, he fell."

"A likely story," Caitlyn said.

"I'm serious."

"Was the wolf hitting on you?"

"It was Tyler's cousin, Miles."

"Dodging my questions means yes, Miles was hitting on you. And yes, something is going on with you and your boss."

I didn't know what to say, so I said nothing.

"You're a big girl, Betty. And this Tyler Bronson would be a great catch, but be careful. He's older than you, and there's a huge power imbalance. Just look out for yourself."

I knew Caitlyn was right, but I didn't want to face reality right now. I wanted to stay in the fantasy, but deep down, I knew she was right.

The odds of this working out for me weren't good. I heard the front door open, and the kids yelling for their dad.

"I've got to go. It's dinnertime," I said to Caitlyn.

"Be careful."

"Okay," I said, looking at my reflection in the mirror. My hair was a wreck.

51

TYLER

As the day at the office progressed, my mood turned sour.

I'd never thought of myself as a type of person who gave a damn what other people think, but it felt like everyone was staring and snickering at me. Everyone being privy to my personal business felt like an invasion.

I drove home wondering what Betty thought of last night. Was she regretting it? Had she seen the story?

Last night I was sure that I was in love with Betty, but how could that be?

We'd only known each other for a couple of months, and my limited history with women proved I didn't make great choices.

And sleeping with an employee didn't scream smart choices either.

I took a deep breath and centered myself before entering the house. I'd made a pledge when I became a

THE NEW SINGLE DAD BILLIONAIRE

dad that I wouldn't take my bad mood out on the family.

I opened the door, and the kids came running out of the playroom to greet me. It always felt good to come home to their smiling faces. Betty followed behind them at a careful distance.

She looked adorable, with her slightly wet hair, no makeup, and casual clothes.

"Hi," I said, not being able to think of anything else.

"Hi!" She smiled, but it wasn't her big smile that made her eyes crinkle in the corners. She'd probably seen the stories online.

I didn't know what to say, but luckily the kids were busy chattering about their day. Riley told me about school, and Renzo told me about a caterpillar he saw on a plant near the deck.

"You can look, but do not touch," Renzo explained to me as I put him in his high chair.

The children filled any awkward silence during dinner, but I could tell that Betty and I really needed to talk. Betty read stories with the kids while I put the dishes into the kitchen for the maid to take care of in the morning.

After we put the kids to bed, we went into the living room and just stood there in silence. My mind went blank.

"So," Betty started. "This is weird."

"Yeah," I said, hoping to come up with something witty. No luck. "Do you want to have coffee with me out on the deck?" I asked, stalling.

We went into the kitchen together. Betty went to the cupboard to get our mugs.

"I'll prep the machine," I said, not wanting her to make the coffee that I'd invited her to have.

I made Betty a latte and myself a black decaf. We went out to the deck. Betty took a seat by the heat lamp, and I realized we were back in our neutral space. Was it because of the heaters? Or was she giving me a subtle sign that she regretted last night?

The heat lamp provided some light, and I turned on the lights from the pool. I didn't risk turning on more for fear of waking up the children.

Betty took a seat in an armchair next to the heater. My only choice was to take the chair across from her.

I hated that there wasn't a sofa or something we could share on this part of the deck. I made a mental note to buy some new outdoor furniture.

We sipped our coffee in silence, and I felt like I was sinking. Say something, anything, I pled with myself. The awkwardness between us was just too much for me, so I thought I'd just get right to the point.

"Betty, do you regret last night?"

"Do you?" she asked.

I wished she had just answered my question, but I guess it wasn't fair to make her go first.

"I don't, but it feels like things are weird between us," I said.

She nodded. "I feel the same."

"Betty," I said. "Talk to me. Tell me what you're thinking. Something isn't right here."

"Okay, last night was a lot of fun. But I'm questioning whether you have any kind of actual intentions for a relationship with me."

Okay, that was honest and open. Now, how the fuck do I respond to that?

"Last night felt so right. But it feels like everyone is assuming we're a couple and talking about us, and it feels so intrusive."

"So what do we do?" she asked, setting her coffee down on the side table.

I couldn't really see her expression in the dim light.

"Maybe we could go on a date?"

She nodded. "That sounds nice."

"You haven't responded to the Thanksgiving invitation from my sister."

"I didn't know what to make of that invitation. It came before you and I even," she motioned toward my bedroom. "I wasn't sure if they invited me as staff --"

"Absolutely not. They'll have people there for that. They invited you as my date or as a guest. Meredith really likes you, and she really thinks we're a match. Everybody does."

"Do you?" she asked.

The words flew out of my mouth. "Of course I do."

"Me, too," she answered, her voice shaking.

I set down my coffee, got up from my chair, and kneeled in front of her. "Things between us are complicated, but let's take it one day at a time. I think we have something really special here."

She sat up and threw her arms around me. "Okay."

We hugged each other in silence, and then she pulled away.

"But I think Thanksgiving dinner with all of your family is a little too high pressure for the first date," she said.

I chuckled. "Fair enough. What are you doing Friday night?"

"I work Friday nights."

"Something tells me you're going to have Friday night off this week."

We shared a laugh, and I vowed I would make this the best first date ever.

52

BETTY

*O*ur date was for eight tonight, and the babysitter was supposed to get here around six thirty. I wished she was coming earlier. I wanted to look amazing for my date with Tyler tonight, but I had nothing to wear, no time to shop, and almost no time to get ready.

The front gate buzzer rang as I put Renzo into his booster chair for his lunch. I rushed to the door, delighted that the dress I'd ordered online had arrived. I pushed the button to let the truck through the gate and dashed to the door.

When I returned to the dining room with the box, Renzo pointed. "Presents!"

"No presents. It's just a box for Betty," I said. "Look, your favorite. Macaroni and cheese," I said, opening the plastic container that Chef Jerome prepared. It only took a couple of seconds in the microwave. Honestly, Chef Jerome's macaroni and cheese was amazing.

I set up Renzo's fork, spoon, bowl of mac & cheese, apple slices, and carrot slices.

"Aren't you hungry, Renzo-roo?" I asked, encouraging him to eat.

He nodded, and I told him I'd be right back.

I rushed into the room to open the box and see my dress. The moment I opened it, I sensed disaster.

It looked way too small and way too sheer.

I tore off my clothes, put it on and looked in the mirror, hoping that it wasn't as bad as I thought.

It was worse! Even with a slip, the thing was so sheer, and it didn't fit right at all. One of the armpits poofed out all crazy, and the waist hung down at my crotch.

Damn it. I had to pick up Riley from school in ninety minutes, and all the shops in this neighborhood were so expensive. I knew Tyler was going to take me some place expensive. There was no way I could show up in yoga pants or jeans.

Plus, there was no way to cancel this date. We lived together! He'd know I was faking being sick.

53

TYLER

The head of my engagement team droned on, and I tried to focus, instead of daydreaming about my date with Betty tonight. The changes we'd made to our mingles had improved customer satisfaction, but longer-term users complained about the quality of their matches.

I stared at the data, trying to figure out why our algorithm wasn't working. Some of it was because a slew of hookup artists had invaded our app.

Our reputation for having a large base of female users had attracted attention from certain online forums that said we were ripe for the picking.

It was hard to weed these guys out, but we'd instituted robust blocking options and programmed spam features into our messaging app to cut down on the copy-and-paste-Romeos.

We'd reconfigured our match survey a million times, and the results weren't better. I told the team to come up with a new set of survey questions for us to beta test later in the week. Then I wrapped the meeting.

As I left the conference room, Meredith caught up with me.

"Guess who RSVP'd to my Thanksgiving?" she asked.

"I asked her to," I said, opening the door to my office and motioning for my sister to get inside. I didn't want anyone overhearing us.

"So, it's going well between you two," Meredith said. "She was your first match. Maybe the algorithm doesn't need any tweaks."

"Maybe it worked too well. Do you think it's possible that people are being matched with their best match first, and that's why it's not working?"

Meredith shrugged her shoulders. "That's not my department. So are you and Betty officially an item?"

"It isn't as far along as everyone would like to think. We're going out on a date tonight, and," I stopped and looked at my watch. "I want to stop off at the florist on my way home. So I gotta go."

"Flowers. Nice," Meredith said.

I shook my head and left the office. It felt like everybody knew my private business, and I didn't like it.

I stopped off at the florist, grabbed the bouquet I ordered, and headed home. I couldn't wait to see the smile on Betty's face when she saw these flowers.

Tonight's date was going to sweep her off her feet.

THE NEW SINGLE DAD BILLIONAIRE

I'd thought of everything, and even booked the babysitter for overnight.

First, we'll have dinner at Geoffrey's. Then, if the mood was right, we'd go to the Nobu Ryokan Hotel, where Betty could scream her head off without worrying about waking the kids.

When I got home, Betty was still wrapping up dinner with the kids and briefing the babysitter. I gave her the flowers, and she thanked me for it, but she was distracted.

I hopped into the shower. When I got out, Betty was in her room and the babysitter was in the playroom with Riley and Renzo.

I said goodbye and told the kids to be good. There was some whining about not wanting me to leave, but I calmed them down.

After the kids settled with the babysitter, I went into the living room, but Betty wasn't there. Well, I should pick my date up at her door.

I went to her room and knocked.

She popped her head out the door and saw it was me. "I'll meet you in the living room. Let me finish up."

She seemed almost annoyed that I'd knocked on her door, which took me aback.

"Our reservations are for eight," I said.

"Okay, then let me get ready," she said, closing the door.

I went back to the living room and waited. This wasn't the start to the evening that I'd hoped it would be, but when we got to the restaurant, I was sure she'd relax.

She finally emerged from her bedroom at 8:15. She looked beautiful, and I stifled my annoyance.

"Do you like it?" Betty asked.

"Yes, it's great," I said, closing the distance between us and giving her a quick kiss. "Let's get going. We're late."

The driver was waiting out front with the doors open, which saved us some time. Thank goodness Geoffrey's was only fifteen minutes away. When we arrived, we had to wait because our table had been given away.

The annoyance must've shown on my face.

"It's really nice here," Betty said. "I'm sorry about being late. I had to get the kids their dinner, brief the babysitter, and then get ready."

Was she really using work as an excuse? "I had work stuff, too," I said, and then stopped myself before I lost my temper. "But it's fine."

"Maybe the next time we have a date, we can have the babysitter earlier, so I'll have time to get dressed."

Oh, so it was my fault. Interesting.

"Women take a bit of time to get ready," I said, trying to make peace.

We made awkward small talk until the hostess came and took us to a table. When we sat down, I noticed a tag hanging from Betty's sleeve.

I reached into my pocket and grabbed my Swiss

Army knife. "There's a tag on your sleeve," I said. "Looks like you had time to do some shopping."

"It wasn't plan A, but I had nothing to wear. The one date dress that I had was ruined."

There was something about her tone that I didn't like. "I find it hard to believe that you only have one suitable dress, Betty."

"As unbelievable as it may seem, it's true. I haven't done a lot of dating, because I've been dedicated to my work."

"We have that in common," I said.

"I guess so."

This date wasn't getting off to a great start. I needed to turn this around. "How about we get the Malibu Mint Martinis? It's the restaurant's signature drink."

"Sounds good."

I decided to not to sweat the small stuff, and concentrate on us getting to know each other and enjoying Betty's company.

54

BETTY

I took a sip of my Malibu Mint Martini and told myself to relax. The stress of trying to find the perfect dress on a budget in Malibu with two small children in tow had scrambled my brain.

We ordered our meals, and he told me about his work. It was impressive that he built his business from his garage.

"Riley got an A+ on her spelling test today, and Renzo --"

"Let's not talk about the kids. Let's focus on us," Tyler said. I knew what he meant. It was a romantic night out, but he got to talk about his work. Why can't I talk about mine?

I looked out at the water. The view was beautiful; it reminded me of the view from the house.

Not being able to talk about the children made it difficult for me to think of things to say.

"Where did you grow up?" Tyler asked.

"In and around Las Vegas," I said, not wanting to bring up any details. Discussing my childhood wasn't exactly the light, getting-to-know-you conversation people always thought it would be. Before he asked any more questions, I launched into my standard spiel about my life. "I started babysitting when I was sixteen, and I just loved it. That's what started me on my path to becoming a nanny."

"You mentioned that before," he said.

"That's right," I said, remembering that I told him about growing up in the system.

"Do you have any brothers and sisters?" he asked.

I shrugged my shoulders. "Maybe? I don't know."

"Oh," Tyler said, searching for something else to say.

The server arrived with our food and saved us.

Tyler had gotten the surf and turf, and I had ordered the filet mignon. The lobster looked great, but I didn't want to wear a bib or get anything on this dress.

I remembered the tags to my dress were still on the table, so I reached for them.

Tyler stopped me. "Can you throw those away?" he asked the waiter.

"Actually," I said, picking them up and putting them in my purse. "I'll take them."

Tyler looked at me questioningly.

I didn't answer. I was hoping to return this dress when I ran errands on my day off tomorrow. I knew if was wrong, but I really couldn't afford this outfit. It was great that I was getting the night off, but not getting paid overtime like I usually did, made my budget even tighter.

The food and drinks eased the awkwardness between us, and my mood finally lightened. He talked about going to school and his best friend, Nick. I listened, but I didn't have similar stories. I changed schools a lot, and I didn't have many friends.

Tyler told me the story about his sister getting knocked over during a bouquet toss, and how that went viral and helped to get their first million users.

"I remember that! It's crazy. I didn't recognize Meredith," I said.

"She'll be glad to hear it."

"So I guess our viral moment was old hat for you," I said.

"You mean moments. There were two, and no. I hate it. Everybody assumed we were a couple, it puts a lot of pressure on us. And I don't think we need that."

"Yeah, we don't," I agreed, but that it bothered Tyler to have everyone thinking we're a couple was the fact that I filed into the back of my brain.

Since this was our first date, I'd let things unfold naturally, but Caitlyn was right. I needed to look out for myself. "I read online that your uncle is the Bronson grocery store guy. That's pretty crazy."

Tyler frowned. "Meredith and I didn't grow up as wealthy as that part of our family."

"That's another thing we have in common," I joked.

Tyler nodded, but didn't smile.

Had I hit a sore spot? I mean seriously, he just got

done telling me he went to a private school. How poor could they have been?

The second round of martinis erased my judgmental mood. We joked about the night he saw me naked at The Plaza.

"I was so turned on by you that night, that I had to leave and go to bed early because I didn't want you to see how excited I was."

My mouth dropped open in surprise. "That's why you ended the night so suddenly!"

He smiled, looking down at the table. "Yep."

"What a relief! I thought you left because I was an inappropriate drunk."

"Nothing could be further from the truth," Tyler said, his voice sexy and low.

"I guess it'll be handy that the kids will be asleep by the time we get home," I said. Although, the mention of the kids spiked a bit of anxiety in me. I worried they weren't going to get along with the babysitter.

"Well, just in case you are in the mood, I booked a room at a hotel close by. I thought it might be nice to have a night together where we didn't have to worry about waking anyone up."

My mind reeled at the idea. One, I was worried about leaving the kids alone with the babysitter overnight, and two, showing up at a swanky hotel without luggage, screamed that we were having an affair or I was a call girl.

Sensing my discomfort, Tyler put his hand on top

of mine. "But there's no pressure. I'm sorry if I made an assumption. I just wanted to be prepared."

"I'm worried about leaving the children with the babysitter for so long. They've just met."

"She's vetted by the same agency you're with. Besides, they'd never met you before that day. And that worked out," he said.

"That's different. I'm good at my job, and you were there. It can be very stressful for Riley to deal with new adults. Trust comes slowly."

"I know my kids," Tyler said, his fist clenched on the table. "I was just trying to do something nice. We don't have to go. It's fine."

Tyler's cell phone buzzed. He stared at me but didn't move to answer it.

My gut told me who it was. "Pick it up. It's the babysitter, and it might be an emergency."

He got up from the table and headed to the front door to take the call outside, his jaw clenched as he said hello.

The waiter passed by. I asked him for the leftovers to be packed up with the check. "And can you hurry? I think we have an emergency."

Two minutes later, Tyler rushed back to the table.

"I'm sorry, Betty. There's an emergency at home."

Tyler looked around for the waiter. When our server returned with the check and our takeout bags, he shot him a questioning look.

"Your date said that there was an emergency and to get the check," the waiter said.

"Yes, of course," Tyler said, taking out a wad of cash and tossing it into the leather case with the bill.

I stood up. We walked back to the car in silence and climbed in.

As we left the restaurant, I turned to Tyler. "What happened?"

He exhaled and shook his head. "Riley locked the babysitter out of the house."

I nodded my head. She'd tried that the first day I was there on my own.

"Call the babysitter and tell her that the small sliding glass door that leads to the garden is unlocked."

"I guess you do know my kids better than me," Tyler said as he called the babysitter.

I'd thought he'd be more grateful. Tyler Bronson might be great at running his online dating business, but he was a terrible date.

55

TYLER

I woke up feeling like a total jerk. My temper had gotten the best of me, and I'd taken out my frustration on Betty. I needed to make it up to her.

The sound of the kids tromping up and down the hallway told me it was time to get out of bed. I didn't feel like making waffles, so the kids would get cold cereal.

I brushed my teeth, threw some clothes on, and stumbled out into the hallway.

"Good," Betty said, "you're up."

"Betty, about last night. I'm sorry. I was rude, and I didn't properly plan our evening out. What do you say we try it again tonight?"

"Thank you, but tonight doesn't work for me. I have some errands to run, and today's my day off."

She was turning me down!

"You had last night off?" I blurted out, realizing my mistake the second I said it.

"We cut my night off short, and I didn't realize it meant --"

"It doesn't. Of course not. I'm sorry I even mentioned it. Enjoy your day off," I said.

"I will," she said, and then she said goodbye to the kids and left.

Normally, Betty spent her days off with us. She went out occasionally, but most of the time she stayed here.

Damn. I really fucked up.

56

BETTY

My emotions had been all over the place since yesterday. I'd been excited about the date, frazzled about getting the dress, anxious about the cost of the dress, miffed at our date, worried about the kids, and now I was pissed.

I got into my car, seething with rage. Not only had Tyler slept in on my day off, but he wanted to make up last night's horrible date by asking me out on a date with absolutely no notice!

Was he even listening to me last night? I told him I had nothing to wear. Hell, I barely had enough time to return the dress from last night's failed date.

Oh God! I had to go back into that store. I felt so grubby going in there yesterday, and now I had to go back and return the dress.

I told myself that I could do it. It's just a dress at a store for crying out loud. Go in there, return it, and get on with your life, Betty.

THE NEW SINGLE DAD BILLIONAIRE

But as I got closer to the shop, I could feel my stomach churning and my hands shaking.

Having grown up getting all of my clothes donated from charity or at secondhand stores, expensive stores always intimidated me.

Everyone always tells me it's no big deal, and that it didn't matter. I knew they were right, but it made me in a lot of ways just feel ashamed for being ashamed about it. It felt like they never understood. Some people don't comprehend the humiliation of not having enough money.

And Tyler and his family were those people.

I pulled up to the fancy-schmancy store in my old car wearing my cheap clothes to return a dress that the saleswomen knew I couldn't afford.

Embarrassment heated my cheeks as I entered the shop. A girl with dark hair asked if she could help me. She had a cute pixie haircut and a kind face.

"I need to return this," I said, handing over the bag. My voice shook, and I felt ridiculous for being so emotional.

"Not a problem," she said. "Would you like to pick out something else?"

"No, thank you. I just would like you to credit my card."

We walked to the checkout area together.

I took out my credit card and put it on the counter.

She typed stuff into her computer while I avoided eye contact.

"The reason for the return?" she asked.

"I bought it for a date, but --"

My voice shook, and I could feel tears welling up. No, no, no. Please God, don't let me cry in the store.

But it was too late. The tears fell down my face, and it felt like everyone was staring at me.

57

TYLER

$\mathcal{I}$ heard the front door open, and I left the playroom to talk to Betty. As I entered the living room, I heard her bedroom door click shut.

I debated leaving her alone, but the longer things went unsaid, the worse off we'd be. When I got to the door, I heard sniffling.

"Betty!" I called to her as I knocked on the door.

"I'm busy."

"I can hear you crying. Please, let me in."

She didn't answer.

"Please, Betty. Tell me I can come in."

I heard her footsteps. She cracked the door open. She'd definitely been crying. "Everything's okay. Don't worry. See you at dinner."

She started to close the door on me, but I put my foot in the doorway and blocked it.

"You can tell me you need privacy, but please don't

lie and say everything's okay. Because I can obviously tell it's not. Talk to me, Betty. Please."

Her shoulders slumped, and she went back to her bed and sat down on it, leaving the door open.

I took it as an invitation to come in, so I grabbed a nearby chair and placed it next to the bed.

"I'm sorry. I was such a jerk yesterday. Please let me make it up to you. I can get Mick to sit with the kids tonight. He wasn't available last night."

"No," she said, crying harder. "Not tonight."

I didn't understand her. It was as if asking her out again made her angry. "Why not?"

She looked at me like I was insane. "What part of me not having anything to wear yesterday did you not hear?"

I didn't like her tone, but I forced myself to remain civil. "Just wear what you wore last night again."

Tears flooded down her cheeks. She buried her face in a pillow.

"Betty, I don't understand. What's the problem?"

I grabbed the box of tissues off her nightstand and handed it to her.

She took several tissues out of the box, wiped her face, and shook her head. "That's the problem. You don't understand. I returned the dress from last night. I couldn't afford it."

"Why didn't you say anything?"

"I said something. You weren't listening, and it's not an easy thing to talk about. Plus, you never replaced my singular one designer dress. That dress was worth more than my car, and you just never brought it up again. Like it was no big deal."

"Let's go out and buy you a new dress. Several new dresses, and then we'll go out --"

"No. Not tonight. I'm not in the mood to go out on a date. Asking a woman on a date with zero notice is not a good thing. Just because I work for you doesn't mean I'm at your beck and call for dates."

"Betty, it's not like that."

She took a deep breath and curbed her anger. "No, you don't mean it to be like that. But it feels that way."

"Betty, I've been very respectful, but I think you're letting yourself get worked up over a dress and you're taking it out on me."

"Worked up over a dress!" She huffed, tossing the tissues aside and standing up. "First, you were a bad date."

"Listen, I was just upset you didn't acknowledge the flowers and that you were late for our date," I said. "I've got a very important job--"

"I have a very important job. It's watching your kids."

I threw up my hands. "Okay, yes, but I was on time. Now, I understand that giving you an hour to get ready may not be enough time. I get that women--"

"Arranging for the babysitter to show up at 6:30 didn't give me an hour to get ready. You're assuming that a babysitter who has never met the kids can just walk in here and be ready to go for the night. It took almost 45 minutes just to show her around and get the kids used to her. I was frazzled by the time you got home."

I held up my hands in surrender. "Okay--"

She shook her head no and continued talking. "You have no idea what I went through yesterday to get ready for the date. You asked me out with only a couple of days' notice, but I had zero time to buy something. So I ordered a dress online, and it was a disaster. So I took two small children to one of these super expensive shops out here to find something to wear. You know how much money I make, and you know how expensive this area is.

"That's not really my fault."

"You never replaced my one dress, Tyler. And, you've come home late every night, except last night. And then, today, you ask me out again to make up for it with no notice at all."

Guilt seeped in. I kind of understood what she meant by beck and call. I just assumed since she had the day off, she'd want to spend it with me.

"And," she added. "You won't take no for an answer."

"What do you mean, I won't take no for an answer?" I asked, feeling defensive.

"I said no earlier, but you asked me again as if I couldn't possibly not want another date. And now, I'm practically screaming at you and I can't even be sure you understand what I'm saying."

"Daddy? Betty?" Riley's small voice called out from the hallway.

Shit. Riley heard us fighting.

58

BETTY

I felt terrible about fighting loud enough for Riley to hear us last night. Tyler had consoled her, but I could tell that she had been affected.

She'd eaten all her vegetables at dinner and brushed her teeth without being asked. I told her our disagreement had nothing to do with her, but I knew she'd internalized our argument. I used to do the same thing. In some ways, I still did.

Since it was Sunday, it was Tyler's day to take the kids out. I was relieved to have the house to myself, but I didn't dare go out into the hot tub. I didn't want to risk running into him.

I thought about going out for dinner, but I didn't want to wreck my budget. Instead, I heated some leftovers Chef Jerome had prepared and ate early.

Not knowing what to do, I called Caitlyn.

"How's it going with Tyler and the kids?" she asked.

"Okay, how's your work going?" Even though I had

called to get her advice, it felt too awkward to launch into my problems.

"The budgets are unreasonable, the shooting schedule is hectic, and the actors are so good-looking it makes me feel like a troll. It's show business as usual."

I laughed. It was always cool listening to Caitlyn talk about her job. I remembered getting to read some TV scripts before the shows actually aired, and I felt like such an insider.

We made small talk about life in Atlanta, and she updated me on Aubrey's new friends at school. I was happy for her and Aubrey, but I was sad they'd moved on without me.

But that's the nature of being a nanny. It suited me. Sure, sometimes it was sad, but I wasn't great at long-term relationships.

"I take it that things aren't going well with you and Tyler Bronson," Caitlyn said.

"We went on an official date, and it was a disaster. The dress I ordered online was also a disaster, and I had no time to get ready. Plus, he hired a totally new babysitter for the night. It was not good."

"What happened to the kids?"

I remembered that I'd signed an NDA, so I couldn't really give any details about the family. "It's not important, but I just get the vibe that he doesn't understand me. I was so upset, because I had to go to one of those expensive shops near here to pick up a dress," I began, and then I spilled out the entire story.

"You already know my reservations about the two

of you, but this sounds like typical couple stuff. Dudes can be oblivious that way. You gotta spell it out for them."

I sighed. "What if I don't want to spell it out for him? Seems like a lot of work."

Caitlyn laughed. "It is. That's why I'm divorced."

When I hung up, I thought it over. I understood why I didn't have many long-term relationships; they were a lot of work.

But I was regularly talking to Caitlyn, and it felt good. One brief fight was no reason to write off Tyler. When the kids went to bed tonight, I would talk it out with him.

59

TYLER

I took the kids to the toy store at the Brentwood Country Mart, and then Frida's Tacos for lunch. They loved it.

When we got home, Betty was in her room talking on the telephone. I could tell from the dishes that she'd already eaten.

I made the kids their dinner, did bedtime with them, and turned in early for the night. Betty obviously needed her space, and I didn't want to make things worse.

All the next day at work, my situation with Betty consumed me. I did something I'd never done before. I went to my sister for advice.

When I walked into her office, Meredith looked shocked. "You can't fire me. I'm a stockholder."

What the?

"You only go to people's offices to fire them," she explained.

"That can't be true," I said, thinking back.

She raised her eyebrows at me.

Damn. She might be right. I'd stopped calling people into my office to fire them when that one dude burst into tears and wouldn't leave. I shrugged it off. "Listen, I need some advice."

She looked at me like I was insane.

"About Betty."

"Finally!" she said, waving at me to sit down.

I recounted to her what happened yesterday, and she shot me an incredulous look.

"Is it that bad?" I asked. "Because it feels kinda bad at home."

"Do you remember how I cried at Geoffrey's during the engagement party because of what Nick said about my dress?"

"Yeah, that was weird."

Meredith threw up her hands. "No, it's not weird. Women are judged by what they're wearing all the time. You thinking that she should just throw on any old thing and go on a first date at a nice place is ridiculous. And why haven't you replaced her other dress? It was a vintage Roberto Cavalli for crying out loud!"

"Meredith, I've already had this argument with Betty. Can you help me or not?"

"Take her shopping. Or better yet, call Henrietta. She'll handle everything." Meredith grabbed her phone and scrolled through her contacts.

My phone dinged. I pulled it out of my pocket and

added Henrietta as a contact. "So is that your advice? Call this Henrietta person?"

"Tell her you need the works. An entire new wardrobe. Find out a day that's convenient for Betty, and move mountains to get an appointment that day. Do it."

"Do you think this is gonna make a difference?"

"Thanksgiving is in two weeks. She still needs an outfit. Take care of it now. Stop overthinking things and just do what I say for once."

"Is this what I sound like when people call me grumpy?" I asked my sister.

"No. You're way worse."

I chuckled, and I knew she was right. And if she was right about that, she was probably right about Henrietta. Time to make a phone call.

60

BETTY

By the time I got off the phone last night, Tyler was already in his room, either working or sleeping. This morning, he left right after breakfast, and we hadn't had time to talk.

I still needed a dress for Meredith's Thanksgiving. I looked at my budget, and with Christmas coming up, it seemed impossible to find something nice enough to wear that I could afford.

If I had more time, I could probably thrift something acceptable, but between Tyler and the kids, there wasn't time. I could charge something. No, I wouldn't wreck my budget when Tyler still owed me a dress from the disaster at his eMingle event.

Plus, I needed an entire afternoon off to myself to buy it.

When he got home, I was determined to discuss it with him and be firm but polite.

He was late getting home, so we'd already eaten. The kids rushed to greet him at the door.

He hugged the kids and looked over at me.

"We need to talk a little later," I said.

"I was going to suggest the same thing."

I took a shower while he put the kids to bed. I let him do story time and bedtime on his own. It was time that I started taking my nights off, off.

It was important to take time to relax and be alone. It would keep me from being too emotional and too attached to Tyler and the kids.

When I knew that the kids' bedtime routine was complete, I went out to the living room. Tyler was waiting for me.

"Coffee or hot chocolate?" he asked.

"Hot chocolate."

We went into the kitchen, and I let him make the drinks. The two of us went out onto the deck. I noticed the loveseat from the other side of the deck had been moved near the heaters.

I looked over at Tyler.

He shrugged sheepishly as he turned on the heat lamp. "The other chairs are still here. I just wanted to have the option if you felt like sitting together."

His awkwardness made me smile.

I sat down on the loveseat, and he sat next to me. Feeling the hardness of his arm next to mine comforted and excited me. I set my hot chocolate on the table in front of us and turned to him.

He took my cue and shifted his weight so he was facing me as well.

"I wanted to talk to you about the Thanksgiving party," I started.

"Please, don't cancel. I've been doing a lot of thinking, and I'll make sure that you have something fabulous to wear and plenty of time to get ready."

I thought that I'd have to make a big case for having to take time off, and he'd already been thinking the same thing.

I squealed with delight and threw my arms around Tyler's neck. "Thank you! And listen, I'll need to take my days off to find something good this weekend. If you can reimburse me for the dress that got wet at the mingle event, I'm sure I can find something."

Tyler pulled me into his lap. "Actually, I was thinking, we could shop for the dress together."

My gut dropped. It was hard enough for me to shop on my own, but it'd be even harder having someone watch me do it.

"Tyler, I appreciate the gesture, but shopping for clothes isn't fun for me like it is for other women. It's actually kind of," I paused and looked down. Even just thinking about it made my throat tight. "Let's just call it a chore."

"That's why I'm going to help you. It'll be fun."

I highly doubted that.

"Give me a chance," he pled. "Tell me the best day for you, and I'll make all the plans. If it doesn't work, take another day and do it your way."

He looked so hopeful, and I didn't want my insecurities to ruin our newfound compromise. Maybe he was right. "I was thinking about shopping this Saturday."

"Perfect. I'll have Mick take the kids on Saturday, and you don't have to worry about what you're going to wear when we go shopping," he said.

I shot him a look.

"Just be ready for me to make you waffles Saturday morning and the rest will be perfect. I promise. Trust me?"

I didn't know how to tell Tyler that I didn't believe that I could ever trust anybody. "Okay," I said, hoping I wasn't making a mistake.

He leaned down and gave me a toe-curling kiss. His kisses eased my worries. When we came up for a breath, I stood up and took his hand. "The hot chocolate can wait."

Tyler jumped out of his chair and picked me up.

"You don't have to carry me to your bedroom every time," I giggled, as he opened the sliding glass door to his bedroom.

"Next time, I'll give you a piggyback ride."

I laughed, he kissed me again, and I left my worrying for later.

61

TYLER

I woke up with Betty laying beside me in bed. We'd had sex every night this week, so I guess I was out of the doghouse. Today was shopping day, and I wanted to get a workout in to make sure I was calm and centered. Even though I didn't understand why she found shopping stressful, I wanted to be a supportive boyfriend.

The only problem was, I didn't want to wake her up. Sneaking out of bed was a difficult thing to pull off when you weigh 245 pounds.

Betty rolled over. "I'm going to sneak into my room before the kids get up."

"One of these days, the kids are going to catch us," I said.

She smiled and gave me a quick kiss. "But not today."

She threw on her clothes, kissed me one more time,

and then tiptoed out the sliding glass door to avoid the off chance she'd run into Renzo or Riley in the hallway.

I liked that Betty wanted to take it slow before involving the kids. That was the smart thing to do, but I didn't know how much longer I wanted to sneak around.

I hopped out of bed, brushed my teeth, threw on my gym clothes, and headed to the other side of the house to hit the weights.

As I passed Betty's room, I heard her rolling over in bed. Somebody was still tired from last night. I grinned, thinking about it, and then warmed up on the treadmill and hit the weights.

I took a quick shower and got the kids ready. I let them wait in the playroom while I grabbed my coffee and drank it in the living room. M-Forty would be here at 10 AM. Henrietta and her crew would be here at eleven.

Betty had filled out Henrietta's online survey, but she still didn't know about the shopping being here at home. I wondered if making that part a "surprise" was causing her undo stress.

After today, she'd have a whole new wardrobe, and we'd celebrate by going out to dinner.

I'd made a list of restaurants ranging from casual to upscale for her to pick from if she didn't have any suggestions.

I had run my plan by Meredith to make sure I wasn't being "just like a man" about it. Meredith thought it was a great idea and suggested that I give

Betty the opportunity to get her hair and makeup done as well.

She told me Henrietta would have recommendations for me. I didn't think that Betty would care or needed any of that. I'd seen Betty right out of the shower. She didn't need any makeup at all.

But I'd leave that up to Betty. Meredith explained that I didn't understand these things, and judging from how terrible our first date went, I knew she was right.

I may not understand women, but I wasn't the guy who made the same mistake twice.

"Hey, sleepyhead," I said to Betty as she came out of her room. "Did I wear you out last night?"

She blushed. Damn, I love when she did that.

Her face turned serious. "What should I wear for the shopping trip? And don't say anything I want. That's way too vague."

"I'm prepared for this question," I said, standing up. "Let's talk it over while I make you that waffle I promised."

"Tyler, if Henrietta is expecting us at eleven, we should leave soon."

I reached into my pocket and grabbed my phone with my notes from Meredith. "Okay, I talked to Meredith. She told me to advise you to wear clothes that are easy to take on and off. She suggests slip-on shoes, sweatpants, a baggy T-shirt, and the style of bra you would typically wear. "

"I'm going to go into a fancy store wearing sweatpants?"

"Nope. No fancy stores. Henrietta is bringing all the clothes to the house on racks, and everything is going to be in your size. So, you get to sit back on the couch and pick out what you like. You can try things on in your own room, and you don't have to come out if you don't like the way it looks."

"Seriously?" Betty asked. "She's coming over with a bunch of clothes for me to just try on?"

A nervous twinge fluttered through me. "Meredith thought it would be a great idea, and I thought so, too. Did I do alright here?"

Betty launched herself at me and gave me an enormous hug. "That's incredible. I didn't even know people did that."

"Neither did I. So, do you want that waffle or what?"

"I think I'll choose or what," Betty said, pulling me toward her.

I bent down, and the heat in her kiss took me by surprise. My cock immediately jumped to attention. We still had an hour before Henrietta arrived. Absolutely enough time for a quickie.

62

BETTY

Maybe morning sex wasn't such a great idea, but Tyler's competence had turned me on so much. He'd asked Meredith for help and taken notes!

I'd left Tyler in his bed and hurried into Tyler's shower to rinse off so I wouldn't reek of sex while I was trying on clothes. I'd made it a point not to get my hair wet, so all I had to do was jump out and get dressed.

It amazed me that he'd go through all this trouble, just to buy me a dress! I was actually excited about shopping for once, and I forced myself not to feel guilty.

The front gate buzzed. The old-school intercom system made it easy to hear in every room. I listened as Tyler instructed Henrietta where to park so that she could easily wheel the racks into the house.

Tyler entered the bathroom. "Babe!"

"Almost ready!" I said, turning off the water.

I opened the shower curtain and grabbed a towel.

I looked up and saw Tyler watching me with his mouth open in awe.

"Take every shower here," he said with a wolfish grin.

I stepped out of the shower and grabbed my undies. "Tell Henrietta I'll be right out."

"Take your time," he said, smiling.

"I don't want to be rude."

"That's what I came in to tell you," he said, taking the towel from my hand and drying my back. "Henrietta needs about a half-hour to set up, so there's no need to hurry. Plus, I booked her for the whole day, so you wouldn't have to feel rushed."

What a difference from last time!

"Okay?" he asked with his eyebrows raised. He looked adorable.

"I love you," I said, and then I realized what I'd just done! It slipped out. I didn't even know if I meant it. Oh, my God!

63

TYLER

*H*oly Shit! I wanted to let her know she had more time to get ready. I didn't expect that! My heart pounded, and I didn't know what to do. Do I say I love you too?

"I didn't mean it like that," she said, her hand in front of her mouth.

"Then how did you mean it?" I said, growing even more discombobulated by the second.

Betty buried her face in her hands and turned her back to me. She was adorably embarrassed.

The doorbell off the side of the garage rang. Henrietta needed to unload. But I couldn't just leave.

"You've got to get that," Betty said, turning around and pushing me out of the bathroom.

"Wait, Betty," I said, thinking I should tell her I love her, too.

She shook her head. "Go!"

Dumbfounded, I let her push me out of the bathroom.

I walked to open the garage door in a daze, worried that I missed the moment to tell Betty I loved her.

64

BETTY

As Henrietta rolled the racks of clothes into the living room, I went into my room to figure out how I could escape the situation I just created. What made me say that?

Okay, yes, I thought about saying I love you to Tyler. I'd even daydreamed about it while he was at work, but was it true? And even if it was true, I should've let him say it first.

A loud knock on my door interrupted my neurotic thought spiral. "Betty!" a woman's voice called through the door. She sounded like she'd smoked a pack a day since she was nine years old. "We're ready for you."

When I opened the door, she looked me up and down. "You're gonna look fantastic in everything. The hardest part is going to be picking out what you like best. But your man can afford it, so you can have everything and anything. This is going to be fun."

"I only need one dress for Thanksgiving," I said, confused.

Henrietta stopped and looked at me like I was crazy. "Your man ordered the works, which means you're getting a whole new wardrobe."

"I can't let him do that!" I gasped.

Henrietta chuckled. "Wow, you're not much of a gold digger."

"I'm not any kind of gold digger!" I said, realizing how many people must think of me that way.

"Of course not," she said. "But let me give you some advice from somebody who's been there. Sometimes, with rich guys, they have so many lawyers you're lucky to leave with the clothes on your back. Make those clothes expensive clothes." She cupped her hand as if whispering a secret. "Especially the purses. Keep them in their boxes. You can sell them later."

I was about to object, but Henrietta had grabbed me by the wrist and dragged me into the living room.

There were at least sixteen racks of clothing. They had filled the coffee table with tea, crudités, mimosas, and other hors d'oeuvres.

"I didn't know there was going to be food," I said.

"Don't worry," Henrietta said. "There's nothing in there that's filled with salt that's gonna bloat you. And nothing that's going to grease up any of the clothes. But just in case, there are moist towels over there." She waved to a fancy box on the other table.

She motioned to a young man with curly black hair

wearing a white T-shirt and jeans. "We'll start with casual wear, accessories, and shoes."

"Hey," the young man said as he wheeled a rack in front of me.

"This is my nephew, Ephriam," Henrietta explained.

"Isn't this great?" Tyler asked, his face hopeful.

"I thought we were just getting me one dress for Thanksgiving," I said.

"But what happens if we go somewhere for Christmas or New Year's Eve?" Tyler asked.

Henrietta interrupted, "With the wardrobe I'm putting together for you, you won't have to worry about any occasion for practically the rest of your life. Tyler here said you hate to shop. Why drag it out? You've got me. You've got Ephriam. And you'll get all the clothes you can ever need. Sit back and let it happen."

I turned to Tyler, and he nodded.

I sat back and took her advice, and she was right. The hardest part was picking out what I liked best.

65

TYLER

Betty entered the living room wearing a long, sleeveless satin dress. She looked amazing.

"We have a winner," Henrietta said. "You've got to love yourself in this dress. Ralph Lauren never disappoints. The darts in the bust and waist absolutely flatter your figure, and the slit up the back." Henrietta motioned for Betty to turn around. "Sexy yet elegant. You'll wow them at Thanksgiving."

Betty's smile was so wide, her eyes were just slits. "Do you like it, Tyler?"

"I love it," I said.

Henrietta butted in. "His jaw hit the floor the second you walked in here. I will not leave until you say yes to this dress."

"It's a yes," Betty said.

Henrietta's nephew applauded and snapped a digital photo. They explained the pictures were private and that we'd get a copy of them.

Betty left the room to change back into her clothes. I needed to thank Meredith for giving me Henrietta's number. It had certainly done the trick.

"You've got a good one there. She only wanted one dress. With your money, you've luckily found the one non-gold digging gorgeous woman in all of Los Angeles. Don't blow it," Henrietta said to me.

"You know I'm the one paying the bill, right?" I said.

Henrietta laughed.

"I already know the perfect wedding gown for her. And I do maternity clothes, too," she said, winking.

"My sister said you can recommend someone to come to the house for hair and makeup. That's if Betty wants it," I said.

Henrietta's nephew started packing away the clothes that we opted not to purchase.

"I'll email it to you with your itemized bill, and I'll attach photos of all the clothes you kept, along with the designer names. You can use it for your insurance. Should we charge the same card you reserved the appointment with?" she asked.

I nodded yes.

"You know, you absolutely have to take her out to dinner to wear some of her new clothes tonight," Henrietta said.

"I know."

Within a half-hour, I was alone again with Betty. Henrietta was right. Betty was a catch.

Tonight, we would go out to some place special, so I

can tell her how much I loved her. Because I knew, I did.

Betty emerged from her room wearing one of her new casual outfits.

"I feel like going out," she said. "How much longer will Mick have the kids tonight?"

"He said they'd come back around nine, but if I wanted, they'd spend the night with him."

I closed the distance between us.

"We have the whole place to ourselves?" Betty asked.

"Yep," I said, sweeping her into my arms, and giving her a deep kiss.

When we broke from our kiss, she looked up at me. "Maybe we should order in."

I laughed. "Henrietta insisted you needed to be taken out. She isn't the kind of person I feel comfortable crossing. She's great at her job, but she scares me."

Betty laughed. "I appreciated her aggressive friendliness."

My phone buzzed. I gently put Betty back down and checked it. "Speak of the devil. It's Mick. I'll tell him we're taking the sleepover option."

But the second I heard Mick's voice, I knew something wasn't right. Had something happened with the kids? "What's wrong?"

"We had an incident at the park, and the police need you to talk to you. The kids are okay, but they're pretty shaken up," he said.

"What happened?" Betty asked.

"I don't know, but I need to get to the park right away."

66

BETTY

Tyler had been on his phone the entire drive to the park. He hadn't switched his Bluetooth over to the car speaker system, so I only heard half of the conversation.

From what I could gather, the kids were safe but upset. The police wanted to talk to him about "an incident" that happened.

When we got to the park, M-Forty, several police officers, and a bunch of onlookers and photographers were gathered in the parking lot. I didn't see the kids.

Tyler jumped out of the car and ran over to see what was going on. I rushed behind him.

When I got closer to the officers, I heard Renzo crying, but I still couldn't see him.

"You're going to have to step back, ma'am," a police officer said to me.

"I'm the kids' nanny," I said.

The police officer turned to Tyler. "Is she alright?"

Tyler was bent down in the open doorway of a police car. His back was toward us, and he didn't respond.

"That's Renzo crying. I need to see him," I pleaded, feeling helpless.

"I can't let you pass without knowing who you are," the officer stated.

"Mick!" I yelled. M-Forty turned to me. "Tell them I'm okay."

"That's Betty. Let her through," M-Forty said. "The kids need her."

The police officer stepped out of my way.

"Where are they?" I asked.

"We set them in the back of the police car so nobody would try to snatch them again," he said.

Snatch them again!

67

TYLER

*L*istening to Renzo wail and cry out "Mommy!" Nearly broke me.

He'd been absolutely inconsolable. Riley had been stone-faced and quiet. The only thing she wanted was for Renzo to sleep in her room.

I told the kids they could both sleep with me tonight, and they liked that.

Tatiana had tried to snatch them off the playground when a couple of fans spotted M-Forty.

Riley had screamed loud enough to get Mick's attention.

Mick ran over and yanked Renzo out of Tatiana's arms and then called the cops. Tatiana fled the scene.

The police were still searching for her. I'd call my private investigator in the morning.

Renzo had cried for a half hour, sobbing, "Mommy."

He didn't stop crying until Betty picked him up. She held him the entire drive home.

I know I shouldn't be jealous, but it'd been over two years, and Renzo still preferred Tatiana to me. I couldn't console him at all.

I needed to spend more time with the kids and give them more of my focus.

68

BETTY

It'd been several days since the kidnapping attempt. Tatiana, Tyler's ex, hadn't been apprehended yet. Tyler had opted to work from home, and the kids slept with him every night.

I knew he must be so stressed, and I was determined to help him as much as I could.

I woke up early to prepare breakfast and get the kids ready, so Tyler could have some time to himself to work out.

As I was mixing the waffle batter, Tyler came into the kitchen. "What are you doing?"

"I thought I would get the kids their breakfast and help them wake up so you could have some time to work out."

"That's unnecessary," he said, his voice curt.

"It's not a problem," I said.

Tyler's eyes narrowed. "You can finish with the breakfast, but I'll get the kids ready. And don't worry about me having time to work out. I know how to prioritize my children."

"Tyler --"

"Betty, this isn't up for discussion," he said. "And next time you want to change the morning routine, you need to discuss it with me beforehand." Then he walked off.

Sheesh.

69

TYLER

I woke up early to get a workout in before breakfast. I'd been skipping them, and between the stress of Tatiana being at large and working from home, my emotions were getting out of control.

Since Thanksgiving was Thursday, Riley was off from school all week. I made sure that I didn't have any meetings scheduled for the early afternoon, so I could take the kids out.

Plus, I'd booked a surprise weekend at the Disneyland resort for just me and the kids Friday through Sunday.

If Disneyland couldn't bring us together, nothing would.

Things between Betty and me had cooled, and I know I needed to talk to her about it, but for now, she seemed to understand.

Stealing a page out of Betty's book, I exited my

room through the sliding glass doors and walked through the deck to the living room. I found if I walked down the hall, the kids would hear my footsteps and wake up.

When I got to the other side of the house, I ran into Betty, leaving her bedroom.

"Good morning," she said.

"Keep your voice down. I don't want to wake the kids," I said. "Where are you going?"

"I'm getting a cup of coffee. Don't worry, I won't make the kids breakfast or anything crazy."

Oh boy. Here we go. I put my hand on Betty's shoulder. "I need to spend more time with the children. They've been through something traumatic, and they need their father."

"I understand that. I was trying to help you, that's all."

"I appreciate that. But I want them to see me as their primary caregiver."

Betty threw her hands in the air in surrender. "I absolutely understand. You're the father, and I'm their nanny."

"Good," I said, kissing the top of her head and then leaving to work out. This week it would be me and the kids, and everyone was on the same page.

70

BETTY

All I needed to do was get through Meredith's Thanksgiving dinner, which had blossomed from a dinner at their house to some elaborate thing at a country club, and then I could go back to being just the nanny.

I looked at all my beautiful clothes. As pretty as they were, they felt more like payment for services rendered than a gift.

The Tyler who'd been a grump to all of his workers on the night we met was the Tyler I was living with now.

Tyler had been so cold to me lately. I told myself it was because of the attempted kidnapping. It probably was. But maybe it was also because I told him I loved him that same day.

Had I scared him away? Or had I taken what we were doing here way too seriously?

Dads sleep with nannies all the time. I heard so

many of them talk about it at the park. I needed to save my money. Because if everything I'd heard from other nannies over the years was true, I'd be looking for a new job soon.

I did my hair and got dressed. When I went out into the living room, Riley and Renzo were already ready for the day.

"So pretty!" Renzo said.

"Like a princess," Riley added.

"Thank you," I said. "You two are beautiful, too, Riley and Renzo-roo!"

I looked over at Tyler. "You look beautiful," he said, and his voice and facial expression were softer than they'd been all week.

A spark of hope bloomed in my heart, but I tamped it down. A polite compliment didn't mean that Tyler Bronson was in love with me.

"Thank you," I said. "You look very handsome yourself."

As we walked outside, Tyler whispered in my ear. "Do me a favor, though. Don't call the kids Riley-roo or Renzo-roo. That's my thing."

"Of course," I eked out, but my heart was breaking.

71

TYLER

Meredith and Nick had put together an entire mini daycare to look after all the children who came, and the kids loved playing with their cousins. That would leave Betty and me some time to enjoy ourselves.

Betty always looked beautiful, but she absolutely shined in that dress. She'd been so great at giving me a chance to bond with the children. I wanted to spend tonight reconnecting with her.

Betty had been quiet the entire car ride over, but I figured it was because she was nervous. I knew her dress would be a hit, but she wasn't used to going to events like this.

Once the kids were safely ensconced in the play area, I turned to Betty.

"So, what should we do first? Do you want to dance? Get a drink?"

She shrugged. "Whatever you want."

Her voice didn't seem her sunshiny self.

A server walked by with a tray of champagne. I grabbed two. "Your favorite," I said, handing her a glass. "But two is the limit for you," I joked.

"Maybe I shouldn't drink at all," Betty said.

"No, drink it," I said. "I was joking."

Betty put down her drink on a nearby table. "I think I'll grab a Diet Coke at the bar," she said, and then just walked away from me.

What the hell?

72

BETTY

I'd hit my limit of Tyler nitpicking at me. Don't call the kids Riley-roo or Renzo-roo, Betty. Two is the limit for you.

He might be my boss, but he's not the boss of me. I'm a guest, and it's my night off. I could drink the entire bar if I wanted to.

Not that I wanted to.

"I'll have a Diet Coke," I said to the bartender.

"I'll have the same," a man's voice repeated behind me.

I turned to see Miles, aka the Big Bad Wolf, wearing a boot on his foot.

"Oh my God! Are you okay?" I asked.

"Do you know, that's the same thing you said to me when I fell off the curb on Halloween?"

"No," I laughed. "But it sounds like me."

The bartender got us both our Diet Cokes.

"I'd ask you to dance, but." Miles motioned to his foot.

He pointed to a nearby table and looked over at me. "Do you want to sit with me? I can't have anything harder, because I'm on pain meds."

"Sure," I said. "Do you need help?"

"Nah, I've been hobbling around on this thing since Halloween. It'll come off in another two weeks. But even with it off, I'll miss ski season."

He sat down at the table. I'd never been to such an elegant party. They decked the place out in fall colors with large glass centerpieces featuring sunflowers, orange roses, and red daisies, and little pumpkins at the base.

I sat down next to him. "Sorry about ski season."

"It's probably for the best," he said. "I'm a terrible skier."

I laughed.

"Are you sure it's okay to talk to me? I don't want you-know-who to throw me in front of another car."

"You fell, and you know it."

"I backed away from his murderous rage face. It's very intimidating. He's the Hulk minus the charm."

"Well, we all can't be as charming as 'unnamed man,'" I said.

Miles chuckled. "That's the glory of living in Florida most of the year. The paparazzi don't know who the hell you are."

We made small talk, and a familiar-looking man stopped by our table.

"Hey cousin!" Miles said.

"You better watch out. Tyler might see you," he said.

"Even if I broke another foot, it'd be worth it," Miles said, turning to wink at me.

"I'm Aiden," the cousin said. "We met at the Halloween party. I was with my wife, Lauren."

That's why I recognized him. "Nice to see you again."

"I'm going to check on the twins in the kids' area before dinner. Make sure they're not trying to kill each other," he said.

"Uh-oh!" someone said, walking up to Miles and me.

"Hey cousin!" Miles said.

"How many cousins do you have?" I asked.

"Hundreds. We're practically an infestation," Miles said.

"And we're all good looking," the cousin said. "Some of us more than others."

Another man stopped and looked over. "Is this the table trying to piss off Tyler?"

I looked at Miles. "Is this another cousin?"

"Yup," he answered.

"This one is Carter," he said, pointing to the taller one, "and that one is Everett. But don't worry, you'll get them mixed up. Everybody does."

"It's easy to remember me," Everett said. "Everett is easy on the eyes."

"And the most ridiculous," Carter said, rolling his eyes.

"Don't look now, but somebody's glaring at us," Miles said, taking a sip of soda.

"I'm not gonna look, but you can tell me. Is it Tyler?" I asked.

"Oh yeah," Miles said, smiling.

Carter looked at me. "Want to get him really mad? Dance with me."

"I don't want to make anybody angry," I said.

Carter stood up. "Even better. Dance with me because I'm a brilliant dancer. The music's great. And you're at a party."

I was tired of Tyler jerking me around.

"How can I argue with that?" I said, taking Carter's hand. Time to have some fun.

73

TYLER

Betty's laugh made my blood boil. She was dancing with my cousin, Carter, and it took all of my willpower not to go over there and kick his ass.

"Easy," Meredith said, as she came up to me. "Carter's a good guy. He's not trying to home in on your girlfriend."

"I don't know about girlfriend," I said. "Things might've moved way too fast. The kids are already way too attached to her."

Meredith poked my arm. "What the hell are you talking about?"

I pushed her hand away. "You don't understand. Wait until you have kids. Everything and everyone takes a backseat to them."

"You're being an idiot," Meredith said.

"You know what happened a couple of weeks ago."

"Betty won't kidnap your children," Meredith said.

I let out an exasperated huff. "Of course she won't. But after just a few seconds with Tatiana, Renzo kept crying for his mother. He was inconsolable until Betty came along." I shook my head. "I need to take more time to bond with those kids."

"Oh, I get it now," Meredith said. "You're not just jealous of Carter. You're jealous of Betty."

I shot my sister an angry look. "I am not."

"You should ask her to dance before the song is over. You don't want to miss your opportunity with a girl like Betty," Meredith said.

"Gee, you're so deep," I said to my sister.

She shook her head at me and walked away.

I looked over at Carter and Betty dancing. The song was ending, and I knew I should walk over there and ask her to dance. But I just couldn't do it.

74

BETTY

When it came time for dinner, I made up with Tyler. I took my seat next to him and gave his hand a gentle squeeze.

"I was hoping you'd ask me to dance, but maybe I should've asked you," I said.

Tyler looked down at me and smiled. "After dinner?"

"Sounds good. I'll warn you, though. I might not be as light on my feet after turkey and stuffing."

Tyler took my hand and kissed it. Meredith and Nick stood up to thank everyone for coming and tell everyone how grateful they were to have everyone in their lives.

Meredith said they had an announcement to make. "We're having a baby!"

Balloons dropped from the ceiling, and the band played.

Dinner was served. Everybody was happy for

Meredith and Nick--especially M-Forty.

After dinner, the conversation turned to what everyone planned to do for the long weekend. Apparently, Tyler's Uncle William was having people over on Saturday.

Lauren asked me. "Are you two going to come?"

"Betty, go," Tyler said.

"I can't go without you," I said.

"You can bring the kids," Aiden said. "We're bringing the twins."

"No," Tyler said. "I have a surprise planned for the kids. I'm taking them to Disneyland."

"Oh," I said, looking at Tyler. I had heard nothing about it.

He squeezed my hand. "It was a last-minute idea. I guess it's a surprise for you too. You get the house all to yourself with the long holiday off. Or you can go to my uncle's place."

"I don't mind going with you and the children on my weekend off. It sounds like fun," I said.

"Don't worry about it. It's a family trip just me and the kids," Tyler said.

Ah yes. A family trip without me. My heart sank and my ears grew hot with embarrassment. I could've sworn I saw Aiden and Lauren frowning.

"Lucky me," I said. "Three full days off."

The reality of my situation descended on me. I'd been in the tabloids with Tyler for months. One of the stories even mentioned I was the nanny. So everyone knows. Now here I was sitting next to him like a date, but he was announcing to them all I was not going on the family trip to Disneyland.

I was that nanny--the young, naïve nanny sleeping with her boss. And I'd told him I loved him.

How stupid could I be?

A few minutes later, I excused myself from the table, went into the bathroom, and cried.

75

TYLER

I woke up determined to have a great day with my kids at Disneyland. They'd had a great time last night playing with the other kids and eating way too much cranberry sauce and pumpkin pie.

Betty had gotten quiet after dinner. She said she wasn't feeling well and went to bed the second we got home.

I figured I'd talk to her before the kids got up. I hopped in the shower, and when I got out, my phone was buzzing up a storm.

Meredith had blown up my phone while I was in the shower: *I can't believe you! How could you say that at dinner last night?*

You better take Betty to Disneyland!

No, forget it. I'm going to take her to Uncle William's so she can have a good time without you.

I was about to text her when my phone rang.

"What are you so crazy about?" I asked.

"I heard Betty crying in the bathroom last night, and then I talked to Lauren because she was sitting near you," Meredith said.

"Betty told me she was sick last night," I said.

"You're an idiot. You sat there with Betty as your date and then told everyone that you are going to take the kids to Disneyland for a family trip."

"What's the big deal?" I asked.

"You can't bring someone who works for you to a dinner as a date, and then talk to her like she's the help in front of everyone."

"I did no such thing," I said, offended. "You're taking this way too far. I just said I was taking my kids on a family vacation. Just family."

"So you're saying that Betty isn't part of the family?"

"Betty isn't part of the family!" I yelled.

I heard footsteps in the hallway, and my heart dropped.

It wasn't the footsteps of little kids. It was the shuffling of Betty's house shoes.

I hung up with my sister. I needed to explain to Betty what I meant. When I stepped out into the hall, Riley was standing there, but Betty was gone.

"Good morning, Riley-roo! I've got a big surprise for you."

She said nothing. I wondered if Riley had heard me on the telephone.

"I'm taking you and your brother to Disneyland!"

Renzo popped out of his room. "Disneyland!"

Riley looked at me. "Is Betty coming?"

What the hell? I tamped down my temper. Had Betty said something to the kids?

"No, it's just going to be the three of us. I've got a hotel, and we're going to spend the entire weekend there."

"Betty was gonna teach me how to make friendship bracelets, so I could give them to my friends."

"You can do that another time," I said.

Riley stomped her foot and ran into her room. "I don't want to do it another time."

"Riley!" Renzo yelled as he knocked on her door. Riley opened the door for him and shut it again.

That's it. I needed to find out what was going on. What had Betty said to these kids?

76

BETTY

I woke up in the morning wanting to talk to Tyler before the kids got up and before they went to Disneyland. But as I walked down the hall, Riley heard my footsteps and called to me.

I opened her door, and she asked me about the friendship bracelets. I told her that her dad might have a surprise for her.

That's when I heard Tyler on the phone. He was saying something angrily, and then he yelled, "Betty isn't part of the family."

I wasn't sure if Riley heard, but I told her we'd talk about the friendship bracelets later. Then, I ran back to my room.

I refused to cry. There was no reason to. I wasn't a part of this family, and I didn't need to be.

The sharp knock on my door made me jump.

"Betty, I need to talk to you," Tyler growled.

He was mad at me? I stormed to the door and threw it open. "Okay, talk."

"What the hell did you tell the children?"

"Language," I corrected. "And keep your voice down. It's not good for the children to hear you yelling."

Tyler glared at me and then whisper-yelled. "Don't tell me what's good for my children."

I rolled my eyes. "Tyler, I was just reminding you. Riley's already heard us fighting once."

Tyler pushed his way into my room and shut the door behind him. The room felt small, with his giant body and temper crowding the space.

"What did you tell her that made her not want to go to Disneyland?"

"Nothing."

"What were you doing in our half of the house that early in the morning?"

"I didn't realize there was a limitation on when I could be in different parts of the house. You never had a problem with me being there early when we were having sex."

Tyler took a deep breath. "You're upset that you don't get to go to Disneyland, but that doesn't mean you can shit talk to the kids so they don't want to go."

"How could you think I would do that?" I said, keeping my voice down, but yelling as loud as I could in a whisper. "I went over there to clear the air between us. Oh, and I know how you feel about me. I heard you loud and clear on the phone."

"Betty, what I meant by that was --" he paused.

I filled in the blanks for him. "I'm not part of the family. You told me this several times. I'm the nanny who was stupid enough to sleep with you and think that it meant something. I get it. We're not a couple. I'm not in the family. Now, since it's my day off, why don't you go to Disneyland and get out of my room."

77

TYLER

The kids were finally asleep, and I was exhausted. We spent the afternoon in Disneyland, and we had dinner downstairs with Mickey and Minnie. Once they saw the castle, whatever crankiness they'd had about coming without Betty disappeared.

My thoughts about coming without Betty could only be spelled out in one word -- regret. The happiest place on earth is damn depressing when you're fighting with a woman.

Every time the kids squealed with delight over something, I imagined Betty would've loved it.

Not to mention, taking two small kids to Disneyland is a two-person job. I'd definitely taken Betty's childcare skills for granted, and I needed to apologize.

I grabbed my phone and texted her: *Can I call you?*

I grabbed a bottled water out of the refrigerator in

the suite, and sat on the couch waiting for her to text me.

To keep myself from obsessing, I opened my laptop and returned some emails. Four hours, a dozen texts, and three phone calls that went straight to voicemail later, I gave up and went to bed.

Damn, I'd really fucked up.

78

BETTY

I'd powered down my phone the second I got a text from Tyler and kept it off all night.

He needed to learn that he wasn't entitled to my time when I wasn't on the clock.

Plus, I was afraid to hear his apology. It might lure me back into that nebulous situation-ship. Besides, I knew part of the reason he was sorry right now. Did he think he could handle two small children at Disneyland on his own?

It'd be nice to have this big house to myself and some time alone. Even though it was November, it was 74° and sunny out.

After a leisurely breakfast, I changed into my bikini and headed out to the deck, stopping by the refrigerator to grab a fancy flavored water that I'd been too nervous to drink.

I dropped onto a chaise and luxuriated in the sun with my fancy beverage. I debated taking my bikini top off. Topless tanning wasn't my style, but I always hated the tan lines. No, it'd be my luck that there was some sort of camera or something around here. I decided to just lower the straps from my shoulders.

A lazy, kid-free, Tyler-free day by the pool would be perfect. I savored having zero responsibilities and vowed to relax and take this time for myself. Maybe I'd even splurge and get food delivered.

A half hour later, I missed the kids, but I was determined to make the best of the day. I must've drifted off, because I was startled awake at the sound of a woman's voice.

I sat up in my chaise, and my top fell in my lap! I scrambled to put it back on. My mind was a jumbled wreck from being half-asleep still.

"Betty, it's me."

I turned and realized it was Meredith.

"What are you doing here?" I asked, fastening my top.

"You didn't answer the front door, so I let myself in. I came over to take you to the barbecue at Uncle William's house."

"It's my weekend off, and I'm going to relax by this pool," I said. "But thank you for asking."

Even though I was lonely, I didn't want to be even lonelier hanging around a sea of strangers.

"I'm really sorry my brother has been an absolute ass. He's insecure about how attached the kids are to you, and his ex really screwed him up."

My heart went out to Tyler. I'd heard other nannies

talk about parents having a hard time when the kids were too attached. But there was more to my situation with Tyler than just the kids.

"I sympathize with him, but none of that is my fault," I said, stopping to think. "But you know what is my fault?"

Meredith tilted her head and waited for my answer.

"I looked at the situation with Tyler and me through a naïve and overly optimistic lens. I'm going to take this time to reflect on my mistakes and choose the best path forward."

Meredith scooted onto the lower half of my chaise. "That is a great idea. And you can do all of that reflection at the barbecue."

Meredith's phone dinged. She looked down at it and smiled.

"Guess who just texted me saying he thinks he's blown it with you," Meredith said. "He wants my advice."

I felt my heart flutter with hope again. But just because Tyler wanted his sister's advice on how to get me back, didn't mean that he loved me, or that he wouldn't take advantage of me. It especially didn't mean he wouldn't break my heart.

"Tell him he needs to keep things professional, or he's going to lose a nanny."

"Let me guess how you're feeling," Meredith said. "You're feeling used, and you're worried about what everybody thinks of you. I know this one. I've been through this a million times."

Tears threatened. Meredith hit the nail on the head when she said I felt used. "And so stupid. It's such a cliché. I thought I was smarter than this."

"I know he cares about you --"

I held up my hand and forced her to stop. "Don't even go there. If he cares about me, I don't like the way he shows it." I shook my head.

"You're right," Meredith said. "But how long do you think it will take for you to get lonely and cave?"

She had a point. It'd been hard to turn my phone off, let alone keep it off.

"I'll make you a deal," Meredith said. "We'll both ignore my brother for the rest of the weekend. And you'll come with me to the barbecue. I don't want to go alone, and Nick had to fly to New York."

"It'll take me too long to get ready."

Meredith waved me off. "It doesn't start for four hours. We have plenty of time. I know you've got a closet full of fabulous clothes from Henrietta. Come with me."

It surprised me that Meredith's offer tempted me.

"And the best way to combat any type of rumors is for you to walk in there and show everyone that you belong. You're coming as my friend and my guest. And, if it sucks, my uncle's house is only ten minutes away. I'll make sure it costs nothing for you to come back home."

Meredith stood up, took my hand, and dragged me off of the chaise.

"It's settled," she said.

I guess I was going.

* * *

The moment Meredith's driver pulled up to William Bronson's mammoth estate, I felt like I'd made a mistake.

Meredith turned to me.

"I've known these people my entire life, and every time I pull up to this house, I feel like I'm dressed in rags."

I shot her a confused look.

"My side of the family isn't as well-off as theirs. Not by a mile. But don't make assumptions about them like I did for years. They're actually nice. And don't worry about everyone staring at you, because today I'll be the center of attention. I just announced I'm having the new Bronson baby. That makes me the star."

Meredith put on a pair of oversized sunglasses and smiled. It made me laugh.

When we walked into the party, Meredith was right. Everyone was overjoyed at her pregnancy, and it was easy for me to mingle with a few of the cousins I met yesterday and blend into the background.

I was just feeling comfortable when I spotted her. The salesclerk from the shop where I returned my dress! The one I cried in front of!

I told myself that I was just seeing things, but I made my way to the pool area just to be safe.

Tyler's house was amazing, but it was a shack

compared to William Bronson's house. The Olympic size swimming pool overlooking the Pacific Ocean amazed me.

"Hey!" someone said. "Do you remember me?"

I looked up. It was the salesclerk!

79

TYLER

Our second day at Disneyland had been an utter disaster. I couldn't wait to get out of there. Renzo had freaked out on the Pirates of the Caribbean ride, and both kids had sunburns on their feet because I forgot they were wearing sandals.

Cranky from their sunburn, the kids kept fighting. Every time Renzo did something that made Riley mad, she'd sing "a pirate's life for me" and Renzo would cry. Honestly, I loved my children, but I wanted to cry myself. How on earth did Betty do this every day?

Everything about this trip sucked balls, and it was all my fault for not bringing Betty with us. I sighed. I hoped the kids would be in a better mood after their post-lunch nap here at the hotel. That's if they'd settle down.

My mind wandered back to Betty. I checked my phone. She still hadn't returned my texts or calls. Meredith was ignoring me, too.

"Yo-ho, yo-ho," I heard Riley sing in the other room.

"Daddy!" Renzo screamed.

That's it. I couldn't take another day of this. We were going home right now.

BETTY

It turned out the salesclerk from the store was named Lydia, and her father worked for the Bronsons.

"So, what does he do for them?" I asked.

"They call them executive house managers now, but he's the butler."

"Have you lived here your whole life?" I asked.

Lydia nodded. "It's been cool growing up here, because you're around a lot of really cool stuff. But it's kind of weird."

I nodded. "I didn't know how poor I was until I saw all this stuff. It's like another planet."

"Sometimes I wish I just grew up in a normal house. I never knew how expensive everything was until I got older. And it feels like there's this big divide between us and them."

"Yeah," I said. "Although, for a while there, I thought the money difference didn't matter."

"Are you in love with him?" Lydia asked.

"I thought so, but now I'm just embarrassed. Am I that obvious? Do they all think I'm silly?"

"They don't really talk to me about that stuff. I only asked because of what you said when you were crying at the store. I really felt for you, because the same thing happened to me."

"Really?" I asked, and then I noticed Everett staring at us.

Lydia must've noticed that I was distracted, because she looked over her shoulder. The second Everett saw Lydia turn around, he looked away.

"And that's the reason I can relate," Lydia said.

"Is there something going on with you and Everett?" I asked.

"There's never anything going on between me and Everett. Do you want to go up to my room? We can steal a tray of hors d'oeuvres and a bottle of something and have our own party."

I smiled. "That sounds perfect."

81

TYLER

There is no amount of overtime I wouldn't pay Betty to take these kids off of my hands. The second I got home, I'd apologize. Then, we'd put the kids to bed, and everything would be back to normal.

Renzo cried almost the entire car ride home. My driver put up the privacy window, which he never did.

Renzo finally tuckered himself out when we were fifteen minutes from home. It was 7 o'clock at night.

I carried him out of the car and took Riley by the hand. When we got into the house, all the lights were out. Riley yelled out for Betty.

"Is she not home?" Riley asked.

"Maybe not," I said. "Go knock on her door while I put Renzo into bed."

Riley ran off to Betty's side of the house, and I laid Renzo into his bed. Luckily, I'd used Betty's tip about putting the kids into their pajamas for the long car ride home so they could go straight to bed.

Riley came running back. "She's not home."

My heart dropped.

BETTY

*E*ven though Lydia was younger than me, she seemed so much smarter. She'd traveled to Vienna, spoke several languages, and, most impressively, was great with her money.

"Dad always told me. You need an emergency fund and an exit strategy," she explained, pouring some vodka into a half empty plastic container of cranberry juice and shaking it.

"I've been working hard on my emergency fund, but what do you mean by exit strategy?"

"My exit strategy was to go to Vienna to study abroad. When I got back, I realized my crush on Everett was futile, so I've been staying at the dorms at UCLA. Your exit strategy is where you go when it all falls apart. It keeps you from feeling trapped. It empowers you."

That sounded like exactly what I needed. "I don't have one, but I want one."

"Let's do it!" Lydia said, pouring my drink into an old coffee mug and handing it to me.

For the first time since Caitlyn left Los Angeles, I felt like I had a friend in town, and we were going to make the best plan.

83

TYLER

I'd stayed in the living room until after midnight waiting for Betty to get home. When I heard the front door unlocking, I fought the urge to rush over and demand to know where she'd been.

I needed to remain calm, apologize, and work things out.

"Betty!" I called, trying to keep my voice friendly and casual. "Is that you?"

She entered the living room. "I didn't expect you to be home until tomorrow. How was Disneyland?"

I debated lying, but I was honest. "It was a disaster. It was a mistake to not bring you."

"It can be a lot to handle two kids at an amusement park. You'll get the hang of it. What's most important is that the family had bonding time."

That last part stung, but I had it coming.

"About that, Betty. I'm sorry. It was wrong of me to say that, and you absolutely are a part of the family."

Betty held her hand up. "Tyler, we are both going to get better at boundaries."

I didn't like the way this was going. I stepped closer and moved to put my arms around her, but she stepped back.

"No, Tyler. I don't know what we were before, but I know what we'll be going forward. I'm your nanny. You're my boss. On my days and nights off, you'll be on your own. And I'll be taking my two-week vacation during Christmas, so you should make some arrangements."

"Betty, I'm sorry I hurt you. You mean a lot to me. None of this is necessary --"

She cut me off. "Who are you to tell me what's necessary? I work for you, Tyler Bronson, but you don't own me. You don't get to just use me, discard me, and then think you can pick me up again."

"I didn't use you. It was a mutual choice," I said, my temper flaring.

"From now on, I'm choosing not to do that anymore. My reputation as a nanny has probably already taken a hit from it. But if you can't handle it, I'll find employment elsewhere."

Employment elsewhere! My head was swimming. What was happening? What had I done?

Before I could say anything else, Betty turned around, went to her room, and closed the door.

84

BETTY

As I exited the plane, I told myself I'd focus on having fun and not worrying about Tyler and the kids.

When I'd decided to take my vacation during Christmas, I actually had no plans. I just knew that I couldn't bear being home with Tyler and the kids for the holidays.

Then, Caitlyn had asked me to come visit her and Aubrey. Even though I had been their nanny, they treated me like a part of the family.

When I got to baggage claim, I heard a familiar voice yell, "Betty!"

I turned and saw Aubrey. "You've gotten so big."

I ran over to Aubrey and gave her a big hug.

"Thank you for coming," Caitlyn said. "It hasn't been the same without you."

I hadn't realized how much I'd missed them until

seeing them in person. Every nanny says your first family leaves the biggest impression.

I didn't know if that was the case, but I knew that Caitlyn and Aubrey held a special place in my heart. "It's so good to see you two."

"You better grab a space at the luggage carousel before it gets too crowded. People can be vicious around here," Caitlyn said.

We waited for my luggage to come out. When I grabbed the handle, the old latch gave out, and my bag popped open. Of course, the bras and undies that I'd cleverly packed on the bottom of the suitcase so no one would see were the first things that fell out.

No matter how much I tried to prepare, things kept falling apart.

85

TYLER

I thought being in the office would make it easier to not think about Betty, but my mind kept going back to her.

She'd helped me pick out a temporary nanny while she was gone, and she'd been right about not leaving the nanny on his own at the beginning. Tommy seemed like a nice enough guy, but nobody could replace Betty.

Focus. Stop swooning over Betty and fix this algorithm problem. The days in between Thanksgiving to Valentine's Day are the busiest season for dating apps. My idea that we were giving people their best matches too early in the game had helped some, but it still wasn't where I wanted it to be.

Someone knocked on the door to my office, but before I could invite whoever it was in, the door flew open.

Of course, it was Meredith.

"I think I can help with your problem," she said.

"Let's not talk about Betty. I need to work."

"I wasn't talking about Betty, but it's very interesting that you'd assume that. Missing her, are you?"

I sighed. "It's been really hard for the kids --"

"Bullshit," Meredith said. "They love Tommy. He does balloon animals. It's been really hard for you, because you've been an asshole."

I tossed my pen on the table. "Yes, I blew it. There's nothing I can do about it now."

"There's everything you can do about it now," Meredith said. "If this was a business problem, you would attack it with everything you had and wouldn't stop until you got it. Why are you so complacent with love?"

I shook my head. There was no answer for that. So I changed the subject. "What did you come in here for, anyway?"

"The other day, I was in the kitchen and I absolutely couldn't remember why the hell I was there. I just stood in front of the cabinet."

"This is riveting, Meredith, but I've got a faulty algorithm to fix."

"I was getting to that. The entire time I tried to force myself to remember what I'd walked into the kitchen for. But my pregnancy hormones have scrambled my brain."

"And your ability to get to the point."

"So instead of trying to remember, I worked backward. I looked at all the things in the kitchen that I could've come in for, and I realized I needed scissors."

I stared at my sister, refusing to say another word until she got to the point.

"If you can't figure out the problem from the start to the finish, work from finish to start. Instead of you trying to figure out how to get people to be a perfect match, why not work backwards from two profiles that turned out to be a perfect match and figure out what happened?"

"You mean reverse engineer it."

"Exactly," she said. "I emailed you a link to two profiles, where the people were an absolute perfect match. They totally fell in love. Figure out how that worked and use that for the algorithm."

"I'll need more than one couple," I said, opening my email. "Can you get me more people who matched?"

"I'll work on that. But in the meantime, look at those two," she said.

Meredith left, and I clicked on the link to check the data points on the profiles. We stripped the names of the users for privacy reasons and to overcome biases based on names, nationalities and photos.

My phone buzzed. "Mr. Tyler, I have a call from Ben Haberman for you. He says he's Riley's biological dad."

My heart sprang into my throat as I snatched up the telephone.

86

BETTY

*C*hristmas with Caitlyn and Aubrey was low key and cozy. I bought Caitlyn some perfume and Aubrey a new diary. Caitlyn gifted me new luggage, which was perfect, because my suitcase wouldn't survive the trip home.

"We got it all queued up, Betty," Aubrey called from the living room.

I grabbed the last bag of popcorn out of the microwave and headed to the living room to settle into a nice Christmas movie with my former family.

I joined them on the sofa and handed over our individual bags of my great popcorn. We each liked different flavors.

Caitlyn turned to me. "There is a lot of debate whether this is really a Christmas movie. But I absolutely believe it is. This is the movie that made Sandra Bullock famous."

"I've always wanted to see it," I said, as they hit start on the movie *While You Were Sleeping*.

I watched the movie and caught myself getting choked up when the main character Lucy talked about not having a family. By the end of the movie, I had to excuse myself to the restroom.

It was a light comedy, but there was something about her longing to have a family and then finally finding one that really got to me.

When I stepped out of the bathroom, Caitlyn was there.

"I'm sorry. I didn't even think --"

"No, it was a great movie. I loved it."

"Listen, there's something I wanted to talk to you about before you leave tomorrow. You haven't mentioned anything about your current work situation."

I opened my mouth to speak, but Caitlyn held up her hand. "I have the next couple of months off, and then the new season shoots in April. Don't give me an answer now, but promise me you'll think about coming back as our nanny. I know in a couple of years Aubrey won't need a nanny. But don't you think in a couple of years, you might want to start a family of your own?"

"I was just talking about this with my friend Lydia. I was thinking of saving my money and maybe opening up a daycare."

"It would be easy for you to open one here in Georgia. Things are cheaper out here. And I'll pay you what he was paying you, so you could save enough money."

"I was thinking about going back to Las Vegas to start the daycare, but maybe it'd be fun to be someplace entirely new."

"And someplace where you have people who care about you," Caitlyn said.

I burst into tears, and we hugged each other. "You know," I said, realizing she'd made the perfect offer. "I think it's a great idea."

Caitlyn shook her head no.

I tilted my head. "I don't understand."

"You need to make this choice after you go back to Tyler. Think it over. The best life choices are the ones you choose. Not the ones you run away from."

I nodded.

"Promise me you'll think about it and let me know a month before shooting starts."

"I will," I said.

When I laid down in my comfy, cozy room, I realized I felt safe here. If I went back and talked to Tyler, I might fall for him all over again, hope for some fairytale, and he'd break my heart again.

I wasn't a character in a zany movie. I was a foster kid turned nanny, and he was a billionaire. Before I could talk myself out of it, I grabbed my phone and emailed Tyler, giving him my notice.

87

TYLER

Now that the kids were asleep and the hubbub of Christmas day had quieted down, I had time to sit alone by the fireplace. The kids had loved Christmas. I'd hired professionals to hang the lights and decorations.

I'd gone overboard to distract them from Betty not being here. I even had fake snow out in the front yard. It worked. They loved it.

I made myself a scotch and stared into the flames. How had I fucked up my life so much?

"Daddy," Renzo said.

"Renzo-roo, you're supposed to be in bed."

"I wanted to give Betty a present," he said, bringing me a picture in a popsicle stick frame.

"She'll love it."

"Can you wrap it like a real present?"

"Sure, buddy. I'll do that."

I looked at the picture. There were stick figures of

four people. One big one that I assumed was me, two little ones that I assumed were Riley and Renzo, and another stick figure with wavy brown hair. But underneath it said, mommy.

"Renzo, who is this a picture of?" I asked, pointing to the brown-haired stick figure.

"Mommy."

"Your mommy has short hair," I said.

"Not Bad Mommy, Betty Mommy."

My mind went back to that day his mother tried to snatch him. He was crying for Betty! Not Tatiana!

"Time for bed," I said, picking him up. After I put him back to bed, I went back out into the living room, looked at his picture, and cried.

How could I have ever said that Betty wasn't family?

I woke up in the morning hung over, but determined to figure something out. Meredith was right. If this was a business problem, I'd be unrelenting until I figured out a way to fix it.

Betty was returning home today. I'd come right home after I met with Ben Haberman. My gut churned. If he really was Riley's biological dad, he could stop the adoption.

I had my lawyer check him out, and unfortunately, he wasn't some unfit drug addict. He was a standup guy. Sure, he'd had some hard times and had little money, but if he wanted Riley, he could definitely make trouble for me.

I grabbed my laptop from my nightstand and opened it up to look at the photos Henrietta had sent with her bill. They were dozens of pictures of Betty. I downloaded them all, turned them into a slideshow, and made that my screensaver.

I'd officially advanced to the moody teenager level of pitifulness.

The thought of whacking off to the pics sparked in my mind, but I decided I'd save that for later.

I checked my emails. Betty had emailed me. At first I was excited, but then I read the subject line. "Two months' notice."

I opened the email and read it. She wanted to go back to work for her former family.

A dizzy, sinking feeling rushed through me. I grabbed onto the nightstand to steady myself. This couldn't be happening!

* * *

Tommy had made the kids breakfast. He was a good guy, and I was glad the kids got along with him. It wasn't the same as Betty, but at least the kids hadn't mutinied on him.

There had to be a way to convince Betty to stay. Between this meeting with Ben and Betty coming home, my nerves were frayed. I worried I wouldn't be able to hold it together.

"Can we build another snowman in the front yard?" Riley asked.

"I don't think there's any snow left. You guys have already used it all to make other snowmen," I said.

"Plus, you still haven't cleaned the playroom or your rooms yet."

"After we clean?" Riley asked.

"Sweetie, there isn't any snow left."

"We can use the same snow," she said.

Tommy piped in. "They want to knock down their current snowmen, and then rebuild them."

"That sounds like an LA developer," I said. Tommy laughed.

"Is that what you guys want to do?"

"Yes!" Renzo said. "I have a big stick."

"I'll make sure they don't hit each other with the sticks," Tommy reassured.

"If you guys do your chores, then knock yourselves out."

The kids rushed into the playroom to clean. I figured it was a good opportunity to talk to Tommy.

"Betty is coming back today, but she doesn't start work officially until January third. I just wanted you to know, so you weren't taken by surprise when she shows up."

"I know. She texted me."

"Good."

"She also mentioned that she was leaving in March or sooner. She suggested I apply for the job, but I wanted to let you know I don't do live-in nanny work full time. But if you need a nanny to work days and some nights, I'd be interested."

"Good to know," I said.

I grabbed my keys, left the house, and forced myself

to keep it together. When I pulled into the parking lot of the McDonalds on PCH, I gave myself a pep talk.

I needed to keep my cool during this discussion, and not commit to anything. It was important to keep things casual, but honestly, I'd be willing to pay any amount to get this guy to go away.

When I walked in the door, a tan man with dark brown hair and brown eyes that were shaped exactly like Riley's looked up at me.

I made it a point to take my time getting to the booth. "Ben Haberman, I presume," I said, holding out my hand to shake hands.

"Tyler Bronson, I recognized you from your pictures on the internet. Plus, Tatiana always said you were huge," he said, shaking my hand.

He had a firm handshake, but we both knew I could take him in a fight if it came down to that.

He motioned for me to sit down, and I slid into the booth.

"You're probably wondering why I asked you here," he said.

My heart pounded in my chest. I nodded, but didn't say a word. He'd have to tell me what he was thinking.

No matter what, I would keep my cool and figure out a way to keep my family together.

88

BETTY

I hopped into an Uber and told myself that I'd stay strong. No rose-colored glasses. No hoping he'd change.

I would create a new life for myself without Tyler Bronson.

But as we got closer to home, I found myself excited to see Tyler and the kids. I missed them.

Even the idea that in my mind I called Tyler's house home was a problem.

"Is there a code I need for the gate?" the driver asked.

"Just pull forward, and lower my window," I said, scooting over to the other side of the back seat.

The driver pulled forward. I typed the code in, and the gate opened. I thought I saw something in the bushes, but it must've been a bird. Because it was gone.

"These Christmas decorations are amazing," the driver said.

"Yeah, they are," I agreed, spotting the children on the lawn playing in fake snow.

Tommy was on the front lawn with them, but he was on the telephone.

The kids had sticks, and they were decapitating a couple of snowmen. I couldn't help but laugh, but that's when I saw her.

She was just a blur of short dark hair and skinny limbs, but I knew it was Tatiana!

"Stop the car!"

"Don't worry, I can take you all the way to the door," the driver said.

"Stop the car!" I yelled. She was only a few yards from Renzo!

89

TYLER

I drove home relieved about the situation with Ben and worried over what he told me about Tatiana.

He'd turned out to be a decent guy. He only wanted what was best for Riley. Ben thought it was best that she stay with her little brother, but he wanted to meet me first.

Tatiana told him that as Riley's biological father, he could block the adoption and extort me for money. When he told her he didn't want any part of it, she'd gone berserk.

He told me that Tatiana claimed she knew where I lived.

Even though I knew we had security cameras and gates, I wanted to call Tommy and let him know to be on the lookout.

The second I left Ben, I called.

THE NEW SINGLE DAD BILLIONAIRE

Tommy picked up, but I couldn't hear what he was saying. I hung up.

He called me a few minutes later. "Can you hear me now?" he asked.

"Yeah," I said.

"We're in the yard doing the snowmen," he said. "The reception is poor out here."

"I know I've told you about this before, but I want you to keep an eye out on the children. I've gotten word that their mother knows where I live, and she's tried to snatch them before."

"Would you like me to call the security company and have them send someone over as well?" Tommy asked.

"No," I said. "I'll be home in a couple minutes."

"Sounds good," Tommy said. But just before he hung up, I heard a kid scream in the background, and Tommy yell, "No!"

The thunk of his phone hitting the ground shot electric terror through my entire body.

90

BETTY

That woman needed to be stopped at all costs.

There was no time to waste. I opened up the car door and jumped out.

Adrenaline pounded through my body. I don't even know how I stayed on my feet, but I hit the ground in a flat-out run.

She turned and saw me. Her eyes looked crazy, and she had something in her hand. She kept running toward the kids.

Renzo screamed.

Something had distracted Tommy on the telephone. When he heard the screams, he noticed, but he was too far away.

I couldn't feel my legs, but I pounded my feet into the ground, trying to launch myself closer to her.

When I got within a few feet from her, she was just about to grab Riley. I lunged at her, grabbing her by the shoulders and throwing her away from the kids.

My body hit the ground, and I slid into the fake snow. I scrambled to get up, and she ran toward Renzo.

Riley hit her with the stick.

"Riley! Get your brother! Run inside the house!" I yelled. Tommy rushed over.

"Call the police! Take the kids inside!" I yelled at him.

Tommy grabbed the children and hurried them away.

"My babies!" the woman howled.

I tackled her again. I saw something metal in her hand. Was that a gun?

I made a fist and punched her in the wrist and forearms over and over again until she dropped whatever it was.

The woman recoiled in pain as my fists flew at her. My ears pounded with blood. I heard a low-pitched rumble, but I didn't know what it was.

Someone was grabbing me from behind. I swung my fist behind me. It struck something squishy.

"Betty!" a familiar voice shouted.

My arms were held down at my sides, and I realized Tatiana was limp on the ground next to some kind of tool. It wasn't a gun. It must've been something she brought to bust into the gate.

Tyler kneeled in front of me. "Are you okay?"

Blood dripped from his nose. I must've punched him!

91

TYLER

Tons of police cars and an ambulance had come to the house. They'd cuffed Tatiana and taken her away to the hospital.

The paramedics were taking care of Betty. Tommy had taken the kids into the playroom to calm them down. My nose had stopped bleeding, and I was talking to an officer.

"So you came in when the two women were on the ground fighting in this foam," the chunky officer said. I think he was the one in charge.

"It's fake snow, but the kids have been playing in it for five days, so it doesn't look the same."

"I saw the sign on the gate saying you have surveillance cameras on the premises. Can we look at the footage now?"

Still in a daze, I agreed and took the officer in charge inside. His two subordinates followed.

Once I loaded up the footage, we all watched.

Tommy was on the phone, probably with me, and that's when Betty's Uber pulls in.

When the gate opened, Tatiana slipped through. She must've been hiding in the hedges.

Tatiana tore across the lawn, heading for the kids. Even though I knew the kids were safe here with me, it terrified me to watch it.

The gate opened slowly, and it took the car a few seconds to pull into the circular driveway. The driver drove to the right, which was in the opposite direction of the children. My jaw dropped open when I saw Betty leap out of the car.

"Did she just jump out of a moving car?" the senior officer asked.

"She absolutely did," the bald one confirmed.

"Look at her run," the short officer said.

We all watched as Betty flew across the lawn and leapt to grab Tatiana just as she was trying to put her hands on Renzo.

"Ooh!" both officers exclaimed as Betty crashed to the ground.

Riley hit Tatiana with a stick. Tommy grabbed the kids and took them away. Then, I drove up in my car and pulled Betty off of Tatiana.

"Remind me never to mess with your wife," the portly senior officer said.

"She's not my wife," I said.

"I'd marry her if I were you," he said.

"If only she'd let me."

The chubby cop turned to me and scoffed. "Nobody

goes through all of that for someone they don't love. Whatever problems you've got, fix 'em. Because if you're gonna go through life with somebody, you want somebody who'll fight for you like that."

He was right. Betty had to love me, or at least the kids. And I was going to fight to keep us together as hard as she just did.

92

BETTY

Every muscle in my body screamed with pain. I struggled to get out of bed, not knowing how long I'd slept. I went into the bathroom, but I didn't have any ibuprofen there.

This afternoon felt like a bad dream. After the police left and the adrenaline wore off, I came into my room to unpack, but I must've fallen asleep.

I didn't even know what time it was.

I brushed my teeth even though my entire shoulder ached. I would probably have to go to the doctor tomorrow.

Maybe there was some ibuprofen in the guest bathroom.

I checked my phone. It was one o'clock in the morning. I'd slept for five hours.

I wanted to change my clothes, but it hurt too much. The guest bathroom. Get to the guest bathroom.

I stumbled down the hall. The lights in the living room were off, but the fireplace was lit.

"Betty," Tyler called out to me. "Is that you?"

"Don't mind me," I said, continuing to the guest bathroom. "I'm just going to the guest bathroom to look for some ibuprofen."

I knew if I talked to Tyler, I would fall apart, and he'd hold me with his muscular arms.

No, I needed to be strong.

I shuffled as fast as I could toward the bathroom, but I could hear his footsteps behind me.

"Betty, let me get it for you."

"That's okay," I said, waving him off, but he was already behind me. He put his hand on my shoulder.

"Wait!"

I turned and looked up at him. It felt like we'd been apart for a million years, but I knew things between us would never work.

"Betty, thank you for what you did today. I don't know what we would do without you. You can't leave. I don't know what I would do without you."

I shook my head no. I couldn't fall for this. "The kids like Tommy --"

"The kids love you."

I could feel my resolve slipping.

Tyler gently put his fingers under my chin and lifted my face so that we were looking into each other's eyes. "I love you. I love you so much it scares the hell out of me, Betty. Please don't leave. I don't mean just for the kids. I'll do anything to prove to you how much I love you."

Tears poured from my eyes, and when Tyler kissed me, no matter how hard I tried to stop it, hope filled my heart.

93

TYLER

Betty's soft lips against mine soothed my frayed nerves. But I needed to take care of Betty, not myself. She needed to know how much I loved her, and I needed to win her back.

Tears streamed down her face, and I picked her up and brought her to my bed.

"I'll get you some water, and some medicine for the pain," I said. "Just rest. I'll take care of you."

I dashed to the kitchen to get a bottled water, ran to her room to pick up her pajamas, rummaged through the medicine cabinet in the guest bathroom to grab all the pain meds, and ran back to her in my bedroom.

When I entered the bedroom, Betty was staring at my open laptop.

"I went to turn on the light, and I jiggled it," she said.

This morning I had been so out of it, I left it open on the nightstand.

"They are all pictures of me," she said.

THE NEW SINGLE DAD BILLIONAIRE

"Yes," I said, walking over to the bed to give her the medicine and water. "I missed you."

I held up the two different pain medicine bottles, and she pointed to the white one.

"How many?" I asked, opening the bottle.

"Three."

I doled out three pills, opened up the bottled water for her, and handed both to her.

When she'd taken her medicine, I showed her the pajamas.

"It must be uncomfortable sleeping in the clothes you wore on the plane and --" I stopped, not knowing how to describe it.

"Fighting in the yard," she said.

I chuckled.

"What do you say I run a warm bath for you, so you can relax? Then we'll put you in these PJs, and you can get some more sleep."

She nodded yes, and I helped her out of her clothes and into a warm bath.

Betty needed to know that I'd take care of her for the rest of her life. But I'd start with just tonight.

94

BETTY

Tyler helped me out of the bath. My sore muscles had relaxed, and the pain meds seemed to do their job.

I reached for the towel, but Tyler grabbed it instead. He toweled off my hair and dried the rest of my body. He grabbed a robe off the back of the door and slid it on me.

"Sit," he said, pulling out a little stool from under the counter.

He pulled out a blow dryer from a drawer under the sink.

"Are you really going to blow dry my hair?" I asked.

"I will if you sit down."

"You've got a really nice hairdryer," I said, admiring it.

"Don't leave, and I'll buy you a thousand of them."

I knew he was joking, but my heart sped up just hearing him asking me to stay.

He opened his medicine cabinet, grabbed two spray bottles, and sprayed them in my hair.

"We can't have you getting heat damage," he said.

"You have better haircare products than I do."

"Not anymore. These are yours, and I'll get you more tomorrow."

"No, it's fine."

"No arguing. Or I'll shoot you," he said, turning on the hairdryer.

Our eyes locked as he blow-dried my hair. The heat from the dryer and his stare made my heart speed up. Every time his hands grazed my neck or touched my hair, my excitement grew. When he finished blow drying my hair, I was practically breathless. He put down the blow dryer and helped me off the stool.

The bathrobe had loosened while I was sitting, and the top half hung open. His gaze drifted downward, and when he looked back up at me, I saw the hunger in his eyes.

Sleeping with Tyler Bronson would only make it harder for me to leave. But I couldn't help myself. I wanted him. Even if this was the last time.

I undid the bathrobe and let it fall to the floor. Tyler's eyes grew wide, and within seconds, he carried me back to his bed.

95

TYLER

When she'd slipped off that robe, a part of me wanted to bend her over the sink and take her right there. But that was just my dick talking. My heart wanted to show Betty how much I loved her.

I carried her to the side of the bed, turned down the comforter with one hand, which wasn't easy to do, and then lowered her into the bed.

I stripped off my clothes as I went to the other side of the bed and slipped in beside her.

She turned to me, her eyes wide. I leaned over and kissed her gently. Our kisses deepened, but I kept the pace slow. I wanted to savor this moment.

She moaned.

I continued with a slow, steady, loving pace. Kissing her. Stroking her.

"You're so beautiful, and you feel so good," I whispered into her ear as I reached between her legs.

"Tyler!" she cooed.

She reached down and touched my cock. I groaned. "Easy," I said. "I want to make this last all night."

"Baby, yes," she moaned.

We took our time making out and caressing each other until neither of us could stand it any longer. I reached into my nightstand, pulled out a condom, and slipped it on.

Betty kissed me as she got onto her knees and then climbed on top of me. She straddled my waist, and I positioned myself at her entrance. We stared into each other's eyes as she lowered herself onto my cock.

"Oh God," I said, my eyes drifting from hers down to her body. She looked absolutely amazing on top of me.

Slowly, she worked herself up and down. I grabbed her by the hips and helped steady the pace.

She leaned back and moaned, her eyes closed, mouth open.

"You are the sexiest woman I've ever seen. I want to make love to you for the rest of my life," I said.

Her eyes opened, and she stared down at me. I could tell she was surprised and not sure she believed me. But I was determined to show her I meant it.

I held her by the shoulders as I rolled us over. In one swift motion, she was underneath me.

My maneuver took her by surprise. I smiled, but then my thoughts turned very serious. I leaned close to her, tenting my hands around her.

"You don't know if you can believe me. But I'm

gonna show you, Betty. I'm going to show you how much I love you with every part of my body, every part of my soul, and every action I take every day for the rest of my life."

I could see her expression soften, but I knew she still doubted me.

I moved in and out of her. We both were so excited, I knew we were close. Her hips bucked to meet mine, and I reached down and stroked her clit with my thumb.

"Tyler!" she said, her voice taking on a sense of urgency.

I picked up the pace. She tightened around me. "So close," I groaned.

Her forehead furrowed and her mouth opened as she tensed her leg muscles.

"Yes! Like that!" she hissed.

Her excitement pushed me to the edge. "Betty!"

"Yes! Tyler!"

We both peaked within seconds of each other. I stayed inside of her a few seconds longer, and then I held the base of the condom as I pulled out.

I collapsed next to her, breathless with my heart thudding inside my chest.

Betty rolled over onto her side to face me, and I did the same. Looking at her felt so intimate. "I love you," I said.

"I love you, too."

My eyes widened, and my heart high-jumped into

my throat. I pulled her to me, and I fell asleep with her on my chest. But when I woke she was gone.

96

BETTY

I'd put on the pajamas that Tyler had brought me and gone to my room. The kids would be up soon, and I didn't want them to find me in Tyler's room. Although they were still so young, I couldn't be sure whether they knew what it meant.

Last night had definitely confused my plans. How was life with Tyler and me supposed to work? Was I his nanny, or would I be his live-in girlfriend? If I became his girlfriend, what would I do for a living?

I remembered what Lydia said about an exit plan. If I was Tyler's live-in girlfriend and not getting paid, if he broke up with me, I'd have nothing.

Well, I would have the expensive handbags that Henrietta insisted I buy. That wouldn't be enough. And if Tyler broke up with me after the spring, I would lose the opportunity to go back to work for Caitlyn.

Why had I slept with Tyler? Why had I told him I loved him?

A loud knock on the door startled me. "Betty! Are you in there?" Tyler yelled.

"Yes," I said, rushing to get to the door. "Take it easy. You'll scare the children."

"When I woke up, you weren't there. I thought you were gone. I thought I'd lost you," Tyler said. His voice shook and tears fell from his eyes.

He reached out and hugged me. He hugged me so tight.

97

TYLER

After my freak out, Betty went back to sleep. She was still tired from her trip and yesterday's commotion.

When I'd woken up and thought she was gone, I knew I couldn't live without her.

I knew exactly what to do, but I needed help. I called my sister.

"Is everything okay? Tatiana didn't come back, did she?" Meredith asked.

"No, the police have her at the hospital or something. That's not what I called you about," I said.

Meredith listened as I told her my plan. "Am I crazy?" I asked.

"Absolutely insane. But that's what love does. I'll help you plan the party, but if you want Betty to come, invite Lydia."

"Who's Lydia?"

"She's Uncle William's butler's daughter."

"Send me her number, and I'll make sure she comes. Actually, you make sure she comes. You're better at that kind of thing."

"You're right. I'll take care of the party. The rest is on you."

I hung up with my sister and vowed to make everything perfect for New Year's Eve.

98

BETTY

I racked my brain trying to come up with a clever New Year's resolution to share. The party had been fun, and I was glad that Tyler had invited Lydia.

It was a casual affair with friends and an infestation of cousins. I could tell that Lydia and Everett had been circling each other all night.

I had no room to criticize. I didn't know what to do about Tyler and me. We'd been getting along really well lately, but would it last? We hadn't known each other for even a year.

"One minute until the ball drops!" Meredith said.

I guess I'll just go with the cliché 'exercise more' as my New Year's resolution, since I couldn't say my New Year's resolution was to figure out if I was going to leave Tyler before spring came.

Tyler's hand touched the small of my back, and I turned to him. Damn, he was so handsome.

THE NEW SINGLE DAD BILLIONAIRE

"Are you ready?" he asked. He was smiling so big. I was glad that I wasn't a party pooper. When he originally talked about having people over, I wasn't on board.

Everyone chanted 10-9-8 until we reached one and yelled in unison, "happy new year!"

Tyler swept me into his arms and pulled me into an old-school Hollywood kiss with the dip and everything.

When he pulled back upright, everyone oohed and aahed.

My cheeks flushed.

"Time to announce our New Year's resolutions!" Meredith said, tapping on a champagne glass with a spoon. "I'll start. My New Year's resolution is to drink again once I have the baby."

Everybody laughed, and she took a sip of her sparkling apple juice.

"My New Year's resolution is to actually upgrade to being a named man in the next tabloid story about me," Miles yelled.

A few people gave some genuine resolutions, and then it came to me.

Inspired by Miles's resolution, I said, "My New Year's resolution is to not be a meme this year." I said.

Everyone laughed, and I felt like I belonged.

"It's the host's turn now," Meredith said after everyone went.

"I've got a big one," Tyler said, reaching into his coat

pocket. When he got down on one knee and opened the box, I had to fight not to fall over.

My face and my entire body felt like it was on fire.

I hadn't seen this coming. It was so sudden. I opened my mouth to say something, but nothing came out.

Oh no! I was ruining everything.

99

TYLER

Betty looked terrified. I knew she was going to be shocked, but I didn't want her to feel so put on the spot.

"Betty," I said. "Don't worry. You don't have to say anything."

She tilted her head, but her breathing slowed to something almost resembling a normal pace.

"I'm just going to share my New Year's resolution. I know it's too soon for you to say yes, but it's not too soon for you to say no."

Everybody laughed. Betty relaxed.

"So please, say nothing. Don't answer at all."

I reached into my other pocket, pulled out a necklace, and took the ring out of the box.

"My New Year's resolution is to prove to you I'm a man worth marrying and to propose to you every day. But you never have to answer," I said, stringing the ring onto the necklace and putting it around Betty's neck and then continuing. "On the day you feel you can believe me, just take the ring off the necklace and put it on your finger. And if that day never comes, you can keep the ring. It's worth a fortune."

Everyone laughed.

I stood up and gave Betty a sweet kiss on the forehead. Everyone applauded, and I raised a glass. "Happy new year!"

Everyone said happy new year, even Betty. I knew I'd convince her one day.

100

BETTY

I woke up next to Tyler on New Year's Day. Last night felt like a dream, but when I looked at that giant diamond sitting on the nightstand, I knew it was real.

Tyler rolled over and wrapped his arms around me. "Bethany Abel, will you marry me?"

I wanted to say yes, but something held me back.

"Don't answer. You'll spoil the fun," Tyler said. "I'm supposed to ask you every day until you're certain. We can take our time."

I smiled. He was crazy. I checked the time. "I better get up and get dressed before the kids wake up."

"You can if you want to. But I had the maid put some of your clothes in my closet. It doesn't matter if the kids see you in here. They'll get used to it soon enough."

With that, Tyler got up, put on his workout clothes

and headed for the gym. I stayed in his room the next few nights, and the kids didn't seem to care.

When Monday morning came around, Tyler went to work, and it surprised me to see Tommy come in for work.

"What are you doing here?" I asked.

"Tyler hired me. He said I needed to be here for the transition."

"What transition?"

Tommy shrugged his shoulders and went to tend to the kids.

What the heck was going on? Tyler and I needed to talk.

101

TYLER

Tomorrow was Valentine's Day. I had roses coming first thing in the morning. A romantic boat ride complete with a serenade by me planned for the afternoon. I'd been practicing the ukulele all month. And then I'd top it off with a candlelight dinner on the deck at home, where I'd ask Betty to marry me again.

I loved proposing to Betty every day. It made me feel like I had a purpose. Every day, I wanted to be worthy.

Meredith waddled into my office without even knocking. The baby was due in three months, and Meredith reveled in wearing flats and maternity clothes.

"Has she said yes yet?" Meredith asked.

"It might take some time. But I think she's coming around."

"Have you reversed engineered those perfect couples yet?" She asked.

"Yes, and it's helped, but not quite."

"You should take a closer look at the very first profiles I sent you," Meredith said, smiling.

"Why?"

"Because they're yours and Betty's profiles. That's your data points. The algorithm matched you guys first, remember? You were perfect for each other.

I opened the profiles again and looked at the male answers. Looking at it now, I guess the profile could have been mine. But this wasn't how I would've filled it out.

"No wonder it didn't work. You filled out my profile for me, and these aren't the answers I would've given."

"Well, those are the answers you should've given. Because I was right, you were wrong."

Betty had said she got her profile as a gift. I called her really quick to see if my hunch was correct.

"Are you going to be late?" she asked.

"No, I'm just getting ready to leave, but I had a question for you. Did you fill out your own profile when you subscribed to eMingle?"

She paused. "Honestly, no. Caitlyn did it for me."

I laughed. "Meredith filled out mine."

"They did a great job," Betty said.

"I'll see you soon," I said, hanging up.

I looked at my sister. She knew what I had figured out.

"It worked better because the people who knew you well filled out your profile for you," Meredith said.

"I thought I knew what I wanted, but --"

"The people who love you know what you need," Meredith said, turning to leave. "I love being right."

When I got home, the kids rushed to greet me at the door. Betty was behind them.

"You're right on time," she said, smiling.

When I walked through the front door and saw Betty, something looked different about her, but I couldn't figure out what it was. We ate dinner, and the kids were especially well-behaved. I worried that something in the house was broken.

When Riley finished her food, she turned to Betty. "Mom, can I be excused?"

My jaw dropped open, and a lump formed in my throat.

"You're excused," Betty said, smiling.

"Can I go, too, Mommy?" Renzo asked.

Betty nodded.

When the kids were out of earshot, I looked at Betty. "Where did that come from?"

"Riley asked me about it this morning. I told her it was okay. You don't mind, right?"

I shook my head no as I sniffled, a few teardrops slipping out the corners of my eyes. That's when I noticed what was different.

Betty wasn't wearing her necklace. She was wearing her engagement ring on her finger!

I couldn't speak as I rushed over to her and looked at her hand close up to make sure it was real. I looked into her eyes, but I could barely see anything, I was crying so much.

"Yes," Betty said. "Yes."

102

BETTY

When I woke up on Valentine's Day, I heard a ruckus in the living room.

I threw on some clothes and went out to see what the commotion was.

"Go back into the room," Henrietta yelled at me. "We're not ready for you."

Tyler smiled and rushed over to me.

We both went into the bedroom. "What's she doing here?"

"Helping you pick out your wedding dress for September."

He gave me a kiss and then looked into my eyes. "I love you, Betty Bronson."

Betty Bronson! I loved my new name--my new family name. I looked up at Tyler. "I love you, too."

"I'm ready for you now," Henrietta yelled from the living room.

"We better hurry. She still scares me," Tyler said.

"You," Henrietta said, pointing at Tyler, "out. It's bad luck."

"Don't worry," he said, "you'll have backup."

"Surprise!" Caitlyn said, popping out from behind one rack. Lydia and Meredith jumped out from behind another rack.

"Oh my God!" I said, rushing to hug everyone. Tyler had invited my friends.

After our greeting hugs, I hugged Tyler and thanked him. Then I realized I was a person with family and friends. The hope in my heart had turned to happiness.

Tyler kissed the top of my head and turned to leave.

I stopped him. "Wait! Why do you want to get married in September?"

"It was the earliest I could book the Grand Ballroom at The Plaza."

The Plaza! We were getting married at The Plaza!

Betty and Tyler are getting married at The Plaza, and you're invited!

Join the Sparks Fly Romance VIP Reader Club (https://sparksflyromance.com/bronson5) and get your free bonus wedding scene! Plus, you'll get more great stuff like special sales notices, free books, and behind-the-scenes insider info! And it's all free!

A NOTE FROM THE AUTHOR

*H*i there! It's Tina Gabor!

Thank you for reading *The New Single Dad Billionaire*. Tyler and Betty's story was so fun to write. I've loved single dad romantic heroes ever since I watched *The Sound of Music* as a kid. Christopher Plummer and Julie Andrews! How could I not?

If you've read the other books in the Bronson Billionaire series, you'll notice some familiar places and faces. Geoffrey's is an actual place, The Hollywood Roosevelt (I performed in the Cinegrill Theater there - brag, brag) and I've been to that McDonald's on Pacific Coast Highway so many times. You know, because I'm classy like that.

And speaking of performing, the new host in the dating scene, Christy, is me making a cameo in the book in my attempt to be like Kurt Vonnegut and Stan Lee.

TINA GABOR

FYI: Tina Gabor is a pen name. I write mysteries and do standup as Christy Murphy. I chose the last name Gabor because of Eva Gabor and the Gabor sisters. But I'm digressing.

Back to billionaires!

There are so many stories in this world I can't wait to tell you. Miles, Lydia, Carter, and Everett will be back. William Bronson gets his own second chance romance, and I'm thinking about telling the story about M-Forty and Angela.

So many books to write!

Just in case you've missed some stories in the Bronson Billionaire World you can read about them in the previous books: Aiden and Lauren (Book 1: *The New Billionaire Boss*), Mackie B and Damien (Book 2: *The Billionaire's Faux Fiancée*), Carolyn and Bradley (Book 3: *Four Weddings and a Billionaire*), and Meredith and Nick (Book 4: *Rebounding with the Billionaire*).

If you'd like to read the stories as I write them, or you've got some work to do and want to virtually co-work with me (yeah, it's a thing), join the Sparks Fly Romance VIP Reader Group https://sparksflyromance.com/bronson5/ for details or follow me on my socials. (Links below)

I'd love to keep in touch. Let me know who's story you'd like to read next. Right now, Lydia is the frontrunner, but you never know.

. . .

SOCIALS:
- facebook.com/sparksflyromance
- tiktok.com/@bookpublishingsisters
- instagram.com/sparksflyromance
- bookbub.com/profile/tina-gabor

ACKNOWLEDGEMENTS

Thank you to David, Robb Fulcher, Edie, Briana G, Tiffany, Laurie Reads Romance, Lox on Books, Danika Bloom, Daisy Knox, Giselle at Xpresso Book Tours, Tanya at Read Love Review, RhondaRooo, Christine at Iron Canuck Reviews & More, Reading tonic, D Dent, Magali146, Antonella N, Tracyah, Jeanne R, Sasha, Ricky and all my fellow "flow-ers" at Flow.Club, and real life Tyler.

ABOUT THE AUTHOR

Tina Gabor lives in Southern California with her fiancé and a stray cat named Fred. She loves reading and writing contemporary romances.

- facebook.com/sparksflyromance
- tiktok.com/@bookpublishingsisters
- instagram.com/sparksflyromance
- bookbub.com/profile/tina-gabor

ALSO BY TINA GABOR

Bronson Billionaire Romance Series

The New Billionaire Boss

The Billionaire's Faux Fiancée

Four Weddings and a Billionaire

Rebounding with the Billionaire

The New Single Dad Billionaire

Printed in Great Britain
by Amazon